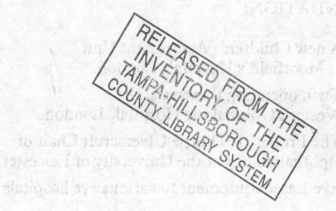

NURSE AT THE CEDARS

The old gentleman had only two weeks to live when Dr. Scott Murdock gave him a new wonder drug. Then it looked like he might pull through—and Doctor Scott and Nurse Susan began to find they had more than medicine in common. But when greedy relatives, who expected their rich uncle to die, found him convalescing instead—real trouble rocked the little island!

Books by Peggy Gaddis
in the Linford Romance Library:

NURSE'S CHOICE
EVERGLADES NURSE
CAROLINA LOVE SONG
NURSE AT THE CEDARS

PEGGY GADDIS

NURSE AT THE CEDARS

Complete and Unabridged

CEN

LINFORD
Leicester

First Linford Edition
published May 1989.

British Library CIP Data

Gaddis, Peggy
Nurse at the Cedars.—Large print ed.—
Linford romance library
I. Title
813'.52[F]

ISBN 0-7089-6686-1

Published by
F. A. Thorpe (Publishing) Ltd.
Anstey, Leicestershire

Set by Rowland Phototypesetting Ltd.
Bury St. Edmunds, Suffolk
Printed and bound in Great Britain by
T. J. Press (Padstow) Ltd., Padstow, Cornwall

1

A STUDENT nurse came swiftly down the corridor to the nurses' station where Susan Merrill stood chatting with Jane Leslie, who was on duty there.

"Excuse me, Miss Merrill." The student nurse was big-eyed with the importance of the message she was bringing, and there was even a note of sympathy in her voice. "Mrs. Thorpe would like to see you. *Right away!*"

Susan smiled and nodded. "Of course. Right away."

The student nurse returned her smile and scurried away.

"Poor you!" Jane looked up at Susan from her charts. "Now what have you been up to?"

Susan spread her hands in a little gesture that acknowledged her ignorance of an answer and said quickly, "I'd better find out. *Right away!*"

"Right away it is when Her Majesty issues an order," Jane agreed as Susan turned and went swiftly down the corridor to the door that bore the legend, "Mrs. Thorpe: Supt. of Nurses."

Mrs. Thorpe, a tall, angular woman who wore her iron-gray hair in an uncompromising bun, her eyes sharp and gray behind her horn-rimmed spectacles, looked up as Susan entered.

No hint of a smile cracked the stern visage, nor was there any warmth in the steely eyes as she said curtly, "Come in, Merrill, and sit down."

Her eyes went back to the chart before her, and Susan perched uneasily on the edge of a chair, her hands tightly folded lest they should tremble in the presence of this woman whom all the nursing staff secretly called "Her Majesty." It was rumored that the interns spoke of her as "The Dragon" and were almost as terrified of her as the nursing staff.

Mrs. Thorpe looked up at last, and her

eyes caught Susan perched there watching her with wide eyes, and suddenly, to Susan's amazement, a thin smile touched the lean, equine face.

"Relax, Merrill," said Mrs. Thorpe, and there was a hint of amusement in her tone. "I've had breakfast, and I rarely gobble up nurses before lunch. You are perfectly safe."

Susan flushed, but relaxed in her chair and felt a little easing of her apprehension.

Mrs. Thorpe looked down once more at the chart and then back again at Susan.

"You've been 1202's 'special' ever since his admission, haven't you?"

"Yes, I have, Mrs. Thorpe. Is anything wrong?"

Mrs. Thorpe's blunt finger tapped the chart, and she said dryly, "So much is wrong that I'm sure you know as well as I do the prognosis of the patient, and what his disease is."

"Well, of course, Mrs. Thorpe," answered Susan. "He has subacute bacterial endocarditis."

3

"And the prognosis?" Mrs. Thorpe persisted.

"Recovery in such cases is extremely rare, and Mr. Cantrell is almost seventy."

Mrs. Thorpe nodded. "Good girl!" she said briskly, and Susan glowed at the hint of warmth in the tone. "The patient is being discharged tomorrow, Merrill. The hospital staff has done everything humanly possible for him, and he knows that he has only a short time left. He wants to spend that time at home."

Susan said huskily, "That's easy to understand, isn't it?"

Mrs. Thorpe studied her sharply.

"You've grown fond of the patient, haven't you?" There was now a faint hint of censure in her voice, and Susan was reminded swiftly of one of the rules that had been drummed into her throughout her training: she mustn't become emotionally involved with a patient.

"I suppose I have, Mrs. Thorpe," she answered quietly. "He's a charming man and so considerate and thoughtful and—well, we all like him enormously."

4

Mrs. Thorpe nodded. "Well, he has grown fond of you, too, Merrill. So much so that he wants to take you home with him."

Susan's eyes widened.

"Take me home with him?"

Mrs. Thorpe's rare smile was touched with an unexpected humor.

"Well, we've told him he will require a certain amount of nursing care for the next few weeks, and since he likes you so much he requested permission to have you as his nurse. So you're being given leave to go with him and look after him. That is, unless you'd prefer not to."

"Oh, no, I don't mind at all," Susan answered hastily, still somewhat wide-eyed. "I'm—well, I'm flattered that he likes me that well."

"He seems to trust you more than any of the other nurses he's come in contact with," Mrs. Thorpe explained. "It's important, of course, that these last few weeks of his life be made as pleasant and as free of pain as possible. He lives on an island off the Georgia coast where it is, no doubt, difficult to find adequate medical service. And since he is enormously rich and has only servants in the house to look after him, he wants you to go with him. Permission has been granted, though of course you may refuse if it interferes with any of your personal plans."

"It doesn't, and even if it did, Mrs. Thorpe, the patient's welfare always comes first with a nurse, doesn't it?"

"Ideally, yes." Mrs. Thorpe's smile was faint but understanding. "Very well, then, Merrill. You will prepare to leave with him tomorrow, as soon as he has been officially discharged. He refuses to travel by ambulance and says his own car and chauffeur will be here to drive him."

Mrs. Thorpe made a slight gesture of dismissal and Susan stood up.

"I just wanted to thank you, Mrs. Thorpe—" she began.

Mrs. Thorpe chuckled dryly.

"Better wait and see what it's like living in complete isolation from the outside world before you thank me, Merrill," she suggested. "That will be all."

Susan went back down the corridor to the nurses' station where Jane still sat with her charts, and when she looked up she said as though surprised, "Still all in one piece, Susie? Congratulations! I wouldn't be nosy for the world, but what in blazes did Her Majesty scold you about?"

Susan drawled, polishing her nails on her immaculate uniform front. "Oh, she was just telling me that I'm to accompany 1202 home for a few weeks!"

"She didn't!" Jane gasped.

"She did so! Seems Mr. Cantrell is being discharged from the hospital to-morrow and will require nursing for a few weeks."

"The poor darling!" said Jane. "His last weeks, and of course he wants to spend them at home."

"That's about it," Susan admitted, and then burst out, "Oh, Janie, with all the medical miracles being performed nowadays, and the wonder drugs and skilled technicians, wouldn't you think

7

somebody could have found a cure for endocarditis?"

Jane nodded soberly.

"After all, honey, we're just humans here in this medical profession, and there are an astronomical number of things we still don't know about hearts and what causes them to flare up. Mr. Cantrell's medical history indicates rheumatic fever when he was a kid; and then this productive inflammation of the heart valves. The pitiful part is that if it had been caught in time, his chances for recovery might have been better."

Susan shook her bronze-gold head beneath its saucy little cap, and her brown-gold eyes were sad.

"In a younger man, maybe. But Mr. Cantrell is sixty-eight, and his health has deteriorated badly in the last few years," she pointed out.

Jane nodded. "Until he got so rich he could buy himself some medical miracles, and by that time his body couldn't take them. That last bout of pneumonia just about put the tin lid on."

The two girls were silent for a moment, and then Jane looked up at Susan questioningly.

"Does he know that time is running out for him?"

Susan nodded soberly. "The chief told him yesterday. I think he suspected it anyway, but when the chief made it official he decided he'd like to—face it at home in his own bed."

Jane said soberly, "He's quite a guy, our 1202."

"*Quite* a guy," Susan said huskily, and turned away to hide the mist of tears that filmed her eyes.

Jane watched her as she went swiftly down the corridor to the door that wore the numerals "1202." There was a sign beneath it that said sternly, "NO VISITORS".

She braced herself, put her shoulders back and pinned a cheerful smile on her face before she opened the door and entered the room. It was one of the best rooms in the hospital, as befitted the man who occupied it. But even so it was a typical hospital room. The man who lay propped against his pillows watched her as she came to the side of the bed and put her fingers on his pulse.

"Hello, Susan," he greeted her, and his smile illumined his thin, drawn face and lit his dark eyes that were in such contrast to his silvery white, but still thick hair. "Don't look so forlorn, Susan. I know all about what I've got. Your chief of staff briefed me about it yesterday."

"I'm so terribly sorry, Mr. Cantrell."

His smile was friendly, good-humored.

"Well, don't be, Susan, my dear!" he protested. "After all, I've had a rich, full life, and if this is going to be the end—well, who was it who said that it was just like leaving one room and opening the door into one incomparably more beautiful? I'm going to have a chance to find out, that's all."

"That's very brave of you, Mr. Cantrell!"

"It isn't at all, Susan," he countered. "If I had a large and adoring family that I hated to leave, and who hated to see

10

me go, I dare say I could make quite a production of passing on! But as it is—" He shrugged slightly and his smile deepened. "The Cedars is quite the loveliest place you can imagine. Or at least I think so. I believe you will enjoy being there for a few weeks."

"I'm sure I shall, Mr. Cantrell, and it's very good of you to want me there."

"Must be very dull young men to let a lovely creature like you wander around these corridors without trying to marry her out of hand." Gerard's tone was lightly teasing.

"They're just busy learning to be fine doctors, and there isn't time for anything else," she pointed out and saw, startled, that his smile had faded and there was suddenly a lost look in his dark eyes.

"They're making a big mistake to get that involved in their work," he said after a moment. "I know whereof I speak. It was like that with me after my fiancée drowned. I couldn't take time to think of another woman. I was too busy burying my grief, seeing how much money I could make and how fast."

"Is that why you never married, Mr. Cantrell?"

His smile was back, but there was no gaiety in it.

"I was twenty-seven when it happened, and we were going to be married the next week." He seemed to be speaking his thoughts aloud. "Lillian was an expert swimmer and had gone alone to the beach. She swam into a nest of Portuguese men o'war. Ever see one of them?"

"No, I haven't, Mr. Cantrell. I've never been swimming in the ocean."

He nodded as though he hadn't heard her, continuing to speak his thoughts aloud.

"They're big, bluish-purple things that float along on the surface of the water, and they have long tentacles almost like an octopus but far more vicious. Their tentacles clasp tightly anything that brushes against them and burn like an acid. Lillian was unable to free herself or get back to shore, and she drowned."

"I'm sorry, Mr. Cantrell. Perhaps if you had been able to forget and find someone else—"

He shook his head.

"There could never have been anyone else. I'm a one-woman man, and Lillian was the woman," he said so positively that she knew he did not want to discuss it any further. "What about you, Susan? Do you have a family?"

"Only a married sister who lives in California. I haven't seen her since I began nursing. My mother died when I was ten and my father when I was seventeen. He was a doctor, and I'd always wanted to be a nurse. And the day I was born he had taken out an endowment policy that would provide for my training, so I entered nursing school as soon as I could."

She smiled at him suddenly and made a little gesture of dismissal.

"And there you have the story of my life, Mr. Cantrell; a neat, small bundle that covers the highlights!"

Gerard smiled. "Then there's no one to object to your spending a few weeks at the Cedars?"

"No one at all. Mrs. Thorpe has given me leave of absence."

"According to your chief of staff, who, by the way, strikes me as a very sound man, it need only be for a few weeks," he pointed out. And then, at the flicker of expression that crossed her face and was gone almost before he could be sure he had seen it, he added quietly, "One thing, Susan my dear, we must settle here and now. And that is—there must be 'no moaning at the bar when I put out to sea.' I know, and you know, that I have a malady for which, as yet, science has been unable to guarantee a cure. We both know that this infection is confined to the endocardium, where it results in a productive inflammation, causing vegetation on the valves and underlying ulceration of the tissue. We also know that there is danger of emboli in various parts of the body when small fragments have become detached from the heart valves

14

and are carried by the blood stream through the arteries to lodge in some distant spot. And when one of those emboli reaches an artery and checks the flow of blood—well, you can see, Susan, that I understand perfectly what's happening to me. Your chief was very good and painstaking about explaining it all to me. I demanded the truth and he gave it to me; and I'll always be grateful to him that he did. To have lain here expecting to recover, in spite of all the pain and the fever and the spasms, would have been unbearable. I'd far rather know the truth. At least I can get my affairs in order; and most of all, I can go home!"

The last words came in a tone that made them almost a prayer, and Susan sensed something of the nostalgia that he had so carefully concealed up until now. Suddenly, knowing that he had only a few weeks to live, she wanted very much for him to spend those remaining weeks in the place he so obviously loved.

He looked up at her, and his smile was

once more in place, though there was a deep earnestness in his eyes.

"So you can see, Susan, why I want no tears; no mourning; no long faces around me. It's as though I were leaving on a long trip. I don't have the faintest idea what I'll find on that trip. Maybe nothing at all; maybe another world so much more beautiful than this that I'll be sorry I was so long reaching it. But to me it's an adventure; and that's the way you must look at it, Susan. Promise me that?"

He was so genuinely, so terribly in earnest that Susan made herself smile warmly at him and covered one of his thin, frail hands with hers as she bent above him.

"Of course I promise, Mr. Cantrell! There'll be no sad songs, no weeping—what was that you said about 'moaning at the bar'?"

"You don't know your Tennyson?" he asked, and there was a teasing note in his voice. "Ah, well, I suppose it was the girls of my generation, not yours, who were able to quote Alfred, Lord

16

Tennyson at the drop of a hat. He quoted softly:

> Sunset and evening star,
> And one clear call for me!
> And may there be no moaning at
> the bar,
> When I put out to sea."

"That's beautiful, Mr. Cantrell," she told him huskily.

"Of course," he said as though he found the remark rather absurd "It's Tennyson. You must read him when you reach the Cedars. You'll find him very inspiring."

"If he has inspired you to all this courage and bravery—" she began, but his look silenced her, and she colored faintly and stood erect. "Tell me about the Cedars. It sounds fascinating."

2

IN the morning when Sue came on duty she was startled to see a man standing beside the bed, his attitude towards the patient that of a mother hen with one chick. He was quite the ugliest man she had ever seen in her life: tall, heavily built, his face looking like something that had been molded and then squashed. The large flat nose, the small eyes set close together, the thick, rubbery lips, the iron-hard jaw, the enormous, ham-like hands all added up to a rather frightening picture. But the man was watching her with anxious, almost pleading eyes.

"Susan, this is my very good friend and devoted companion, Stepp," Gerard introduced the man, and there was genuine affection in his voice. "Stepp, this is Miss Merrill, my nurse."

"Good morning, miss," said Stepp, and

his voice was a surprisingly pleasant baritone, though from his size and his ugliness she had expected it to be rough and grating. "I'm sure obliged to you, miss, for taking such good care of the chief. We're all mighty glad that we're going to have him back at the Cedars. We've sure missed him."

"I'm sure you have, Stepp," Susan answered with a friendly smile. "He'll be ready to leave as soon as the rounds are completed."

"I'll wait," said Stepp in a tone that said there could be no possible doubt of that.

Susan checked the patient and was hugely relieved to discover that he had no fever. With this disease fever was invariably present, though there would be occasional days when it was absent, and she was deeply relieved that this day that he was being discharged he was free of it. If they could just get him back home and in his own bed before the fever began, with its usual accompaniment of chills!

The chief of staff, accompanied as

always by his small but devoted retinue, made his rounds and checked Gerard out, smiling pleasantly as he said, "I've briefed your Dr. Murdock at the village clinic, Mr. Cantrell, and he'll be standing by should you need him, though it's not likely you will."

After a few minutes of leave-taking they went on with their rounds. As the door closed behind them Stepp turned eagerly to Susan.

"We can go now, miss?"

"Of course," said Susan. "I'll get a wheel chair—"

"No need for that, miss," said Stepp, who walked to the closet and brought out the very latest thing in folding wheel chairs and set it up. He turned to the bed and gently drew back the covers, as though he were uncovering a tiny baby, and he slipped his arms under Gerard and lifted him from the bed to the chair. He wrapped a light blanket over his knees, stood up and beamed at Susan.

"You lead the way, miss," he said and took his place behind the chair.

Down the corridor, into the elevator, across the lobby and out to the ramp that led from the drive into the Emergency section, Stepp wheeled the chair like a proud parent wheeling his first child.

Beside a sleeky gleaming late model Cadillac, a middle-aged man in smartly tailored chauffeur's garb stood waiting, and as he saw the group approaching he came swiftly to meet them, his face eager and alight with welcome.

"Hello, Sandy, you old scalawag," Gerard greeted him heartily with an outstretched hand. "It's good to see you again."

"It's good to see you, Chief," beamed the man, and put his hand in Gerard's.

"Susan, this is Sandy Jenkins, a good friend of mine," said Gerard. And to Sandy, "Miss Merrill is going with us · Sandy. She's going to be my nurse for a while."

"That's fine, miss. We'll be mighty glad to have you at the Cedars," said Sandy happily, but Susan knew that his

21

whole mind was on the man who sat in the wheel chair.

As Stepp lifted Gerard into the car and Sandy expertly folded the chair, Susan watched them and knew that these men genuinely loved Gerard, not merely as an employer but as a man and a friend. And she was in no way surprised, for Gerard had made friends easily in the hospital, and the entire staff, from the chief down to the lowliest orderly, was sorry to see him go.

Stepp arranged the blanket over Gerard's knees with such meticulous care that Gerard laughed with a trace of impatience.

"Stop fussing over me, Stepp! You're behaving like the fond parent of a newborn infant. I'm much tougher than you seem to think! Let's get going!"

"Sure, Chief, sure," Stepp soothed him as he held the door open for Susan and slipped into the front seat beside Sandy.

The car purred away like a big, cream-fed cat, and Susan heard the deep sigh of utter content that Gerard gave as he relaxed. She gave him an anxious glance, and unobtrusively her fingers found his frail wrist. But he jerked his wrist away, though he softened the gesture with an attempt at a smile.

"Sorry, Susan. It's just that I grew very tired of having my temperature and my pulse and my blood count checked every five minutes these last weeks," he offered an apology. "If just one more white-clad individual comes at me with a treatment tray and a needle big enough to vaccinate a horse, I'm not going to be responsible for my actions!"

Susan laughed. "I'll promise to be very casual and pay you no more attention than you require," she told him. "Tell me about Dr. Murdock and this village clinic."

She had, of course, been briefed on the man and on the care of the patient; but she had long ago learned that to let a man talk freely about something that interested him was the best method of relaxing him.

"Oh, yes, Murdock," said Gerard, obviously relieved that she had changed the subject. "He's a very sound man. Young, about thirty, I'd say; but a very fine physician and surgeon. He bought out a practice on the island when old Dr. Glenn retired and he's established a small but quite efficient clinic and is doing a very good job. You'll like him, I think, and I'm sure he'll like you. He's unmarried, by the way."

His smile lit an impish twinkle in his eyes.

Susan laughed. "Oh, that makes him most interesting to me, since I'm on the prowl for a husband," she mocked him.

Gerard studied her, amused, admiring her from the top of her bronze-gold head with its saucy little cap to the tip of her spotless white shoes, and nodded.

"Yes, of course, a girl like you would have to go on the prowl for a husband." His tone of mockery matched her own. "The wonder is that you haven't had to beat prospects off with a club all these years. How old are you, anyway?"

"Twenty-four," Susan answered demurely. "Just an old maid, Mr.

Cantrell, heading fast toward spinster-hood!"

"Oh, quite," he agreed. "A pathetic sight to see. You're not getting any younger, so you'd better give Murdock the glad eye."

"Oh, nobody's getting any younger, not even a newborn infant," she answered gaily. "I don't let the burden of my years worry me too much After all, I do have my profession you know, so I don't have to find a husband just to get a meal ticket!"

"Well, don't be smug about that, my girl!" Gerard all but snorted. "Having a man to foot your bills isn't quite all there is to marriage! There's a home, children, family solidarity. That's very important."

Susan nodded soberly. "I know, Mr. Cantrell. I've never had it, not since I lost my mother. So I am fully aware of how important it is. It's just that it seems to me it's terribly important to be deeply in love with somebody before you start thinking about getting married."

Gerard nodded, and now the surface gaiety had vanished from his manner.

"Nothing in this world is more important, girl! See that you hang onto that thought!" His tone was very near a command.

Susan led Gerard on to chat, and now and then she caught Sandy's eyes in the rear view mirror above the wheel and saw the anxiety there, as he looked at Gerard, melt away beneath the relief of seeing the man he so obviously loved at ease and relaxed.

It was early afternoon when the car finally reached the bridge that led to the island, and as it ran over the deep, narrow river Gerard leaned forward a little and pointed.

"You can just catch a glimpse of the Cedars from here," he told her eagerly. "There! See? Through the trees there on the bluff above the river."

Susan caught a glimpse of a rosy-colored roof, tall chimneys, the glimmer of white, and then the car was over the bridge and turning north along a broad highway bordered on either side by enormous oaks, their branches the thickness of a man's body and their curtains of silver-green Spanish moss stirring gently in the restless breeze from the ocean.

"The village is south," Gerard explained. "Here on the north there is nothing except the Cedars and a small church that has been here since Oglethorpe's time. Matter of fact, John Wesley and his brother preached their first sermons here in the new world. There's an oak tree that's called the Wesley Oak, because it was beneath it that the Wesleys preached to the first colonists."

They saw it then, a small white church with an aspiring steeple that was enclosed with a low wrought-iron wall. And surrounding it there was an ancient cemetery whose stones had grown dark with the passing of the years.

Gerard's eyes turned away from the cemetery, and Susan felt a small pain at her heart as she saw his jaw harden slightly; but almost immediately he went on, "and just across there a few miles is the site of one of the most violent battles fought during the history of the island: the Battle of Bloody Marsh. I have some books that you may find interesting, giving the history of the island, and I'll have Sandy take you sight-seeing some afternoon when you're off duty."

"It's a lovely place, the whole island," Susan told him gently.

Gerard smiled down at her, and the tautness of the jaw with which he had turned away from the sight of the cemetery softened slightly.

"The loveliest spot in all the world," he answered, and though the words were simple his tone made them a shout of delight. "The one place in all the world I love more than any other. And I'm coming home!"

He looked down at her and lowered his voice so that it would not reach the two men up front.

"I never expected to, you know. Not as long as there was hope I could be cured. But now that I've faced up to the fact that I can't be, ever, I want to come back home. And now I have."

They had come, above the small white church, to a fork in the road, and as the car turned into the one leading east, Gerard went on, his voice now his normal one that reached easily to the men in front.

"The road to the west leads to another island; one of the most famous and exclusive winter resorts along the coast. There's a hotel there where I'd like to take you to dinner. But since that seems out of question, I'll have Murdock take you as my guest."

"Oh, now, please, you mustn't treat me as a house guest or feel responsible for my entertainment, Mr. Cantrell," Susan protested. "Remember me? I'm your nurse!"

But Gerard wasn't listening, for the car had turned in at a long, winding driveway between ancient cedars that led up to a wide, low house that crowned the bluff. Through the trees, on the east, Susan glimpsed the ocean, and on the west there

29

was the sheer drop to that dark river they had crossed earlier.

Gerard leaned forward a little as the car crept up the drive and the house came into full view. It was not quite the sort of house she had expected; it was built of some grayish stone and its windows were numerous and large. It was surrounded by a brilliant splash of color in the blooming shrubbery and vast flower beds that broke the steeply sloping lawn. The lawn had been terraced, and each terrace was marked with a bright fringe of gaily colored flowers.

The house faced the drive, with one wing facing the river, the other looking out over the ocean. And here as the car stopped Susan saw the ocean and the beach clearly for the first time.

The morning was a perfect one, bright blue sky, sun-drenched sea and beach, fragrance of flowers mingled with the salt-tang of the sea, the house sitting so serenely at the end of its double-drive of cedars, all forming an unforgettable picture for Susan as she got out of the car.

The handsome front door stood open, and as they reached the three wide, shallow steps that led up to it, Sandy and Stepp eased the chair up and through the open door and into a big, square reception room, where two women waited eagerly.

The older one, ample in girth, immaculate in a blue and white striped uniform beneath a voluminous white apron, her gray hair screwed into a tight bun at the top of her head, came swiftly forward, and her voice shook as she welcomed Gerard home.

"This is my nurse, Miss Merrill, Elizabeth," said Gerard. And to Susan, "The best cook in the whole country."

"Well, now, Chief, I ain't right sure of that," said Elizabeth, and bridled happily. "Sandy and I brought our girl, Maisie, to help with the housework. Maisie, come here and meet the chief."

Maisie, a pretty girl in her early twenties, came forward shyly, and Gerard greeted her warmly.

31

"Meet Maisie, indeed!" he protested as he held out a hand to the girl. "Why, Elizabeth, are you out of your mind? Maisie and I are old friends, aren't we, Maisie?"

"We used to be, Mr. Cantrell, but that's been a long time ago and I wasn't sure you'd remember me," Maisie answered.

"Remember you? Why, child, how could I forget you? You were a very intriguing little girl! but you've gone away and grown up!"

Maisie laughed. "Well, it's the sort of thing you have to expect, Mr. Cantrell," she assured him.

"Well, I suppose so. And I must say, Maisie, you're even prettier as a teen-ager than you were as a little girl," Gerard told her.

Maisie bristled ever so slightly.

"A teen-ager? Why, Mr. Cantrell, I'm twenty!" she protested.

Gerard studied her solemnly, though that impish, youthful twinkle was in his eyes.

"My, my, that old?" he marveled. "And not a hint of a wrinkle or a thread of gray in your hair, and I'll bet you have your own teeth!"

Maisie was flushed and laughing as she countered his teasing. And then Susan motioned to Stepp behind Gerard's back, and Stepp nodded and said to Elizabeth, "The chief's room is ready, isn't it?"

Elizabeth grew indignant.

"Well, of course it is. Has been since the day he left. Dusted and cleaned every single morning!" Her tone was almost a snap.

Stepp said cheerfully, "Well, don't rustle your bustle, old girl."

Gerard, laughing, raised a frail hand.

"Stop it, you two! I'd hoped that by now you two had become friends and these arguments between you would have ceased."

"Any time I stop arguing with that big lout, that'll be the day!" Elizabeth sniffed disdainfully.

"I think we'd better get Mr. Cantrell

to bed," said Susan pleasantly but firmly. "He's had a long and tiring trip."

"Well, now, that's a right sensible idea," said Elizabeth as though she wished she had thought of it first.

Stepp turned the chair in the direction of a door at the left, and Maisie swung the door open. As Stepp wheeled the chair across the threshold he turned to Susan and said curtly, "I'll take care of him, miss. You needn't bother to come in."

"But, Stepp, I'm his nurse," Susan protested.

"Sure, miss, and all the nursing you want to do when he needs it, that's fine. But putting him to bed and taking care of him is my job," Stepp insisted, and glanced at Maisie. "Better show Miss Merrill to her room and let her get unpacked."

He wheeled the chair into the room and firmly closed the door upon those who stood outside.

"That Stepp!" Elizabeth sighed. "Thinks nobody can do anything for the

chief but himself. Sandy, bring Miss
Merrill's luggage. Maisie, show her to her
room while I see about some lunch. You
didn't stop on the way for any of that
junk they serve in the cafés and hot dog
stands?"

"Of course not! Mr. Cantrell is on a
diet," Susan answered resentfully.

"Well, I just thought maybe you and
Stepp and Sandy might have got hungry
on the way down," Elizabeth answered.
"I'll send a tray to your room, Miss
Merrill, and Stepp will insist on fixing one
for the chief."

She turned and walked away, and
Sandy picked up Susan's luggage and
gestured to Maisie, who smiled shyly
and led the way along the corridor.

Susan looked about her as she was
ushered into a large, charmingly
furnished room with wide windows over-
looking the ocean.

"But this is across the corridor and the
full length of the hall from Mr. Cantrell's
quarters," she objected "Shouldn't I be

35

closer to him in case I'm needed in the night?"

Sandy and Maisie exchanged grins and Maisie said, "Oh, you won't be allowed in Mr. Cantrell's room at night, Miss Merrill, unless Stepp calls for you. He has the small room adjoining the chief's and he's on twenty-four-hour duty there. He is so jealously possessive that the rest of us are scarcely allowed in the chief's room."

Sandy had put down the two bags and left.

Maisie asked, "May I help you unpack, miss?"

"Thanks, no, Maisie, I can manage beautifully." Susan smiled at her, and Maisie smiled back shyly.

"Then I'll go and see to some lunch for you, miss," she said, and went out of the room, closing the door behind her.

Susan touched her fingers to her hair that had been blown by the wind, adjusted her cap, dropped her cape on a chair and went back across the corridor to the door behind which Stepp and Mr. Cantrell had gone.

As she opened the door Stepp turned sharply toward her, his ugly face dark with resentment.

Mr. Cantrell lay among his pillows, sleeping like a baby, and Susan nodded at Stepp as she moved forward to check the patient's pulse and respiration.

Mr. Cantrell's eyes fluttered open and he managed the faintest possible semblance of a smile, though his pulse and respiration hinted that he was desperately tired.

"Hello, there." His voice was low, and Susan had to lean down to hear him. "You don't have to worry about me, now that I'm home and in Stepp's hands."

"I'm not worrying about you," Susan told him with a warm smile. "I'm just doing my job! You rest now and sleep if you can. And if you can't and want a sedative, you may have one."

"Thanks. But now that I'm at home in my own bed I'll sleep without a sedative," he assured her, and relaxed.

Stepp said softly, "You can go now, miss. I'll call you if we need you."

Susan eyed him curiously, amused yet slightly resentful.

"I'm beginning to wonder why he thought it necessary for me to accompany him if you're going to take full charge," she pointed out.

"Oh, the doctors at the hospital wouldn't let him go unless a nurse was with him," said Stepp frankly. "I talked to a couple of them, but they wouldn't believe me when I tried to tell them I was as good a nurse as they had in the hospital. Better, on account of him and me being such good friends, see?"

He walked to the door and held it open for her, and Susan lifted a shoulder in a slight shrug and walked out into the big square hall.

When she reached the room assigned to her Maisie was waiting for her with a tray of appetizing food, and as Susan thanked her and sat down behind the tray that had been placed on a low table beside the window, Maisie hesitated even as she started for the door.

"Miss Merrill, he's not ever going to get well, is he?" she blurted, and above her tremulous mouth her eyes were wide and sick with the knowledge that there was only one answer to her question even before she had put it.

Susan looked up at the girl and said quietly, "His chances are not good, Maisie."

Maisie caught her breath and her hands clenched tightly.

"I've felt it all along," she said huskily. "But when they let him come home from the hospital, I felt like maybe they thought he did have a chance."

"They let him come home, Maisie, because everything medically possible had been done for him and because he was so bitterly homesick," Susan said gently. "They felt that since he had only a few more weeks to live—"

Maisie gasped, "A few more *weeks?*"

"We can't say positively, Maisie. Nobody can!" Susan answered swiftly.

"But the doctors knew that there was no more they could do for him, and so they let him come home. I know you will all want to do everything you can to make his final weeks as pleasant as you can, won't you?"

"Oh yes, miss! Anything! We'd do anything for him! He's—such a wonderful person. We all owe him so much," Maisie stammered.

"Then the greatest kindness you can pay him is to pretend that he is going to recover," Susan said quietly. "He doesn't want any tears, any long faces. So we must be very careful not to let him become upset by any visible signs of our grief and anxiety about him."

Maisie straightened her slim shoulders and tilted her young chin.

"Of course not, Miss Merrill. I'll tell Mom and Dad, and we'll do what we can to keep Stepp in line," she promised. "This will hit Stepp especially hard. He owes the chief so much; more than any of us, though we all have a deep debt of gratitude—"

"Do you know something, Maisie? I don't think Mr. Cantrell would want to think that any of you feel a burden of obligation or gratitude. You are his friends and he loves you all. Anything he has done for you I'm quite sure he did because he wanted to and because he was happy to do it. So let's try to keep things cheerful, especially around him; we can weep for him in private if we like, but we mustn't let him know it. Will you do that, Maisie? And try to get the others to?"

Maisie nodded and even managed a faint smile.

"We will that, miss, since that's what he wants," she promised. "And if we can just keep those—those vultures away—"

Puzzled, Susan asked "What do you mean, Maisie?"

"I mean those two nephews and his niece, the only family he has; and with a family like that, who needs enemies? If they know he is—seriously ill, they'll swoop down like vultures hovering above a dying animal."

"Why, Maisie, what an awful thing to say!" Susan protested, shocked.

"Well, it's true, miss! They are terrible people. All they care about him is what they can get out of him. And if they find out that he is—dying—well, he's very rich and they'll all want to 'protect their interests,' and what a mess that will be!" said Maisie harshly. "If we can just keep them from knowing—"

"But, Maisie, if they are his relatives, his family, haven't they the right to know?"

"Right?" Maisie sniffed contemptuously. "They've got no rights at all because they don't deserve any. We can let them know—afterwards—and save him the worry and bother of having them here during these last few weeks."

She looked at Susan's startled face and went on swiftly, "You don't know 'em, miss. We do! And we all hate 'em! They swoop down here once or twice a year when they want money. The rest of the time they don't even send him a

Christmas card or a birthday present! So let's forget any rights they may have."

"I'm afraid that's not for me to say, Maisie," Susan answered reluctantly.

"If he was back at the hospital, you could keep unwelcome visitors away from him, couldn't you?" pleaded Maisie.

"Well, yes, of course," Susan answered.

"Then believe me, miss, no visitors could be any more unwelcome than those three—harpies! Miss Joyce would probably bring that brat of hers, too. You wouldn't believe what a pest a three-year-old could be until you meet Barbie!"

Maisie was so intensely in earnest that Susan said gently, "Well, it's not my place for me to warn them of the seriousness of Mr. Cantrell's illness, Maisie. That's for the doctor or the lawyer to attend to, unless some of you here want to write or wire them?"

Maisie's eyes were enormous beneath the impact of that, and she gasped breathlessly, "*Us*, miss? Why, there's not one of us that would so much as tell them the time of day!"

She turned to the door and paused to say, "I'll talk to Mom and Dad, and I guess Stepp already knows we are not to worry the chief by pulling a long face and weeping in the corner. I can't imagine Stepp weeping, and with that face of his, you can't tell whether he's sad or being hysterical with joy. Thank you for trusting me, miss. I won't fail you—or him."

She went out and closed the door behind her.

Susan sat for a moment thinking over the conversation, and then she turned hungrily to the well-laden tray. Outside, the warm spring sunshine turned the close-cropped grass of the sloping terraces to emerald, and the flowers that fringed each terrace were a blaze of color. Beyond at the foot of the lowest terrace, the beach was white and marked with the oncoming breakers that rolled in and slipped back, leaving a creamy foam that melted into the sand.

No wonder, Susan told herself as she luxuriated in the view, that her patient had been so anxious to get back to all this. His windows faced the river, and the scene there was just as beautiful, with the tall, very old cedars marching in a straight line up the drive, and standing in groups at the corners of the terraces.

She could not but be curious about the three people Maisie had mentioned as the patient's only family. Two nephews and a niece, Maisie had said. And the niece, whom Maisie had called "Miss Joyce," had a small child. Strange they hadn't been better friends with their uncle and helped to relieve the loneliness of his life these past years. But then, she reminded herself, there were vast number of families who got along so badly together that they were much happier apart, and this could easily be one of them. And, after all, she went on, she was simply the nurse here, and the private, personal, intimate affairs of the patient were no concern of hers.

3

SHE had finished her lunch when Maisie came back to announce, "Dr. Murdock is here, Miss Merrill. He'd like to talk to you before he sees the chief."

"Oh, yes, of course. Thanks, Maisie. Lunch was delicious," said Susan, and went quickly out into the big reception hall.

The man who stood waiting for her watched her as she came swiftly down the corridor and smiled as she greeted him.

"So you're Nurse Merrill." He smiled and held out his hand. "I'm Dr. Murdock, Miss Merrill."

"I'm so glad you are available, Dr. Murdock." She answered his smile with one equally pleasant.

"And I'm delighted that Mr. Cantrell has such a charming and, I'm sure from what the hospital records tell me, such an efficient nurse as you, Miss Merrill," he answered, and indicated a room across the hall from the one occupied by the patient. "I'd like to discuss the case with you before I go in to see Mr. Cantrell, Miss Merrill."

"Of course, Doctor." Susan followed him into a room that was obviously library and study combined, and sat facing him, waiting for his questions.

They came swiftly as he examined the chart he had taken from his medical bag. She was, of course, able to answer each question competently and intelligently, and when he scowled down at the chart, she studied him. He was younger than she had expected; probably not yet thirty. His hair was thick and dark red and cut so short she felt sure he was trying to deny the slight wave it seemed trying to reveal. His brown face was rugged, rather than handsome, and his tall, lanky body looked strong and wiry.

He looked up unexpectedly and caught her eyes upon him, and a twinkle danced in his own eyes, that were gray-green and

47

set well apart above a strong, Roman-esque nose.

"Now that we've taken each other's measure—" he began briskly, and grinned as color flooded her face.

"I'm sorry if I was staring, Doctor," she stammered.

"I'd have been insulted if you hadn't been," he told her frankly. "I like a nurse who wants to know something about the doctor she is going to be working with. It looks as if we have our work cut out for us, doesn't it? With the prognosis the hospital gives us, I mean."

Susan asked swiftly, "You don't agree with the prognosis, Doctor?"

Dr. Murdock cocked an eyebrow at her.

"Let's just say that I don't agree with any prognosis that denies the patient hope!" he countered. "The man is breathing; and to my mind, as long as a patient is breathing there is hope."

"I do hope you are right, Doctor!"

"So do I," he admitted. "There aren't many men like Gerard Cantrell around in this cockeyed, upsidedown world of ours nowadays, and we can ill afford to lose one. Shall we have a look at him?"

"Oh, yes, let's do, Doctor," she agreed eagerly, and stood up to lead the way across to the patient's room.

Stepp let them in, though with obvious reluctance, and Susan said under her breath, her tone sharp, "Don't be an idiot, Stepp. Dr. Murdock has come to examine the patient."

"Seems to me like there's been enough and too much of that already," Stepp grumbled. From the bed, Gerard spoke sharply, and Stepp moved out of the way.

"Well, well, Scott," Gerard greeted Dr. Murdock warmly. "Good to see you, boy."

"And it's pretty wonderful to see you, sir," Dr. Murdock answered, and shook the frail hand that Gerard held out.

Susan, standing at the foot of the bed, saw that Dr. Murdock's fingers were on Gerard's pulse. Gerard himself realized it at the same moment and grinned wryly.

"A little late for that, Scott, my boy,"

he said quietly. "After all, when the hospital let me come home to die, they didn't pull any punches. I know that it's only a matter of weeks, so don't waste your time."

Dr. Murdock accepted the chair Stepp had brought for him and sat beside the bed, studying Gerard carefully as he answered.

"That's something nobody can tell you positively, sir," he insisted. "How many patients have you known who were given a few months to live and then lived for years and saw their doctors buried while they lived to a ripe old age?"

"Not with what I've got, Scott!" Gerard countered and for just the barest flicker of a moment Susan saw something in his eyes that startled her. "You're not quarreling with the hospital's diagnosis, are you? Dr. Willard is supposed to be tops in his field, which is diseases of the heart, you know."

"Oh, no, I'm not quarreling with the diagnosis; just with their statement that nothing more could be done for you! I'm

50

not yet convinced of that," said Dr. Murdock so firmly that Susan stared at him, wide-eyed. And from Gerard's reaction she knew he was as suprised as she.

"Look here, Scott, what are you trying to tell me?" Gerard demanded after a startled moment. "You yourself sent me to the hospital and said I had a form of endocarditis and that your clinic lacked the necessary facilities for a complete diagnosis."

"I know I did, Mr. Cantrell." Scott Murdock was very much in earnest. "And I followed up the hospital's findings. Naturally, since I interned at City General, I knew just how solid and expert the whole staff is. What I am trying to say, sir—"

Gerard's thin, bony face was touched with a light smile.

"What's with this 'sir' business, Scott? Is that the way a doctor always speaks to a patient who is a few years his senior?" His tone was teasing, and Susan saw Dr. Murdock's amused grin.

"Only if the patient is a man to whom

he owes as much as I owe you, sir," he answered with the slightest possible emphasis on the last word. "After all, Mr. Cantrell, I can't forget that it was you who saw me through med. school and saw to it I interned at City General and then established the clinic for me. That rates a great many expressions of the utmost respect and a gratitude I could never express adequately in a thousand years."

Susan saw the faint tinge of color that touched Gerard's bony face. His eyes would not quite meet hers, and she knew that he was embarrassed by Scott Murdock's words.

"Nonsense!" he said bluffly. "If you hadn't been worth it, I'd never have lifted a finger to help you, make sure of that! You can repay any debt you may feel you have incurred by taking the best possible care of your patients."

"That's why, sir, I've been studying up on all forms of endocarditis ever since I made the first X-rays on you. Why, I've been researching and hunting every minute I could spare from my other

52

patients to find something that would give you a remission of this disease," Dr. Murdock said in his quiet, deeply earnest voice, his eyes never leaving Gerard's face.

Gerard studied him with a sudden intentness, and Susan saw the faint flicker of something that could have been hope in his eyes.

"And?" he said after a moment.

"And I've come up with something, sir," Dr. Murdock told him.

"Something the hospital didn't know about?"

"Oh, I imagine they know about it, sir, but it's a new drug, still in the experimental stages, and they would not want to use it until they are more certain about the results and if there are side effects as there are with so many of the new so-called 'miracle drugs.'"

Gerard cocked an eyebrow at him, and that youthful twinkle appeared in his eyes for a moment.

"I see. You're planning to use me for a guinea pig," he accused.

"Only with your consent, sir. I have to have that, and you must think about it very carefully before you agree to allow me to experiment," Dr. Murdock answered.

"You already have this drug?"

Dr. Murdock nodded. "It's a foreign drug, and I've got enough of it for the treatment of one patient. I put it in reserve, of course, until I could talk to you. I was hoping against hope that the hospital would come up with something that would slow up the progressive stages of the disease if they could not cure it."

"I was told at the hospital, Scott, that not more than one case in hundreds of subacute bacterial endocarditis is ever cured, and those have been in people much younger than I am," Gerard pointed out.

"Of course. I know that, sir," Dr. Murdock told him. "But this just *might* be that one chance in a million. It won't guarantee a complete cure, sir. Naturally, I couldn't promise anything like that. It might mean a few more years of life for you, a remission of the disease; not a complete cure."

Gerard turned his head and looked out over the beautiful scene below him: the sloping lawn, the bright flowers, the stately, gnarled old trees in whose branches birds sang and darted about.

"A few more years!" he said so softly that Susan barely heard the words. "A few more years instead of a few *weeks!* It's a wonderful thought, Scott."

Dr. Murdock did not speak but just sat waiting for Gerard to speak again. Finally Gerard turned his head once more and looked into Dr. Murdock's eyes, the words came.

"What are the chances, Scott, with this new drug, whatever it is?"

"No better than fifty-fifty, sir," Dr. Murdock told him with an all but painful honesty. "But that's better than the chance you have now."

"Which is no chance at all." Gerard nodded and looked across the bed at Susan, that indomitable twinkle in his eyes. "What do *you* think, Susan?"

55

Susan made a little gesture that refused any participation in the decision.

"I couldn't possibly help you decide about a thing like that, Mr. Cantrell," she told him swiftly. "It's between you and Dr. Murdock. "I'll do whatever he tells me, of course. That's a nurse's job. But helping a patient to make such a decision is a responsibility I couldn't possibly assume."

Dr. Murdock glanced approvingly over his shoulder at her and then back to Gerard.

"She's quite right, sir. It's up to you and to me to decide. If you are willing to have me try the drug, I'll have to get your written consent, of course, because it *is* purely experimental. It's been used abroad with mixed results. I'm being very frank with you, sir. It may have no effect at all. You may not respond to it. On the other hand, there's a good chance, I honestly feel, that you may. But it is taking a chance, and you must think it over very carefully before you decide."

Once more Gerard turned his head to

look out of the window at the river, narrow but deep, with its black waters silvered now by the warm sunlight; at the trees on the opposite bank, limned against the afternoon sky.

"A few more years," he murmured, "instead of a few more weeks!"

He drew a deep hard breath and winced slightly with the pain of the respiration. After the pain had eased, he managed a smile.

"It's an intriguing prospect, I must admit," he told Dr. Murdock. "Where do I sign?"

"You mustn't, sir, without thinking very carefully about it. There are a lot of implications."

"Are you afraid to use it?"

"No, Mr. Cantrell, not if I have your consent and I'm completely sure that you understand thoroughly all the various implications and prospects—"

"You've told me that, given the drug, I have a fifty-fifty chance to live a few more years," Gerard told him firmly. "I know, because I've had the fact impressed on me by doctors whom I respect and whose integrity and competence I cannot doubt, that now I can survive for only a few weeks. Is there more to understand than that?"

"Only, sir, that you may not respond to the drug at all and it may not help," Dr. Murdock answered. "But I can tell you this. It will not injure you or deprive you of those few weeks! That I can swear! I'd stake my life on that!"

Gerard said after a thoughtful moment, "Then there's really not much to decide, is there? I'll permit the treatment and accept the drug, so show me where I sign. Susan here can be a witness, and if you want more than one Stepp or some of the others can be called in."

Dr. Murdock said, "I'll have the proper papers drawn up for your signature and Miss Merrill's, sir, and bring them with me tomorrow."

Once more Gerard cocked an eyebrow at him.

"Not quite sure I'd agree to be a guinea pig, son?" he mocked.

"I didn't want to take that much for granted, sir. I wanted the decision to be completely yours, and made only after you had had time to think it over carefully," Dr. Murdock answered. Then reluctantly, he added "But there isn't a great deal of time, Mr. Cantrell. If we're going to get started on this drug, we don't want to waste time."

"Quite right, my boy, quite right. Time is of the essence, isn't it? Then come back tomorrow and bring your devil's potion with you so we can get started!" said Gerard, and grinned at them both, a youthful, surprisingly gay grin. "Here I was thinking I was completely resigned to passing from this vale of tears with grace and courage. Now you bring me hope and my mind has come all unbuttoned again!"

"With all my heart, sir, I hope and pray I haven't given you a false hope!" Dr. Murdock's voice was not entirely steady.

"Even if it doesn't work out the way we hope, Scott, it will at least give me something to look forward to," Gerard told him quietly. "And that's very important to me, now and always."

"Then that relieves my mind, sir!" Dr. Murdock smiled at him painfully. "I admit I'd much rather have tried it on someone else first."

"Nonsense! Don't go around wishing you could find somebody who is in worse shape than I am!" scoffed Gerard. "Or maybe you meant somebody a lot younger."

"I meant someone of whom I am less fond, sir," Dr. Murdock admitted frankly as he stood up. "Think very carefully, sir, and tomorrow when I come back, we'll see what you have decided."

"I've already decided," said Gerard firmly. "Bring your papers, boy! We'll sign them, won't we, Susan?"

"If you're quite sure it's what you want, Mr. Cantrell." Susan smiled at him as she walked to the door and held it open for Dr. Murdock.

Stepp brushed past her, irate at having been excluded from the room during the examination and conference, and as Dr. Murdock followed Susan from the room the door closed with a decisive bang.

Susan smiled over her shoulder at Dr. Murdock.

"That was Stepp, Mr. Cantrell's personal bodyguard and defender," she explained. "He resents my presence here bitterly, so I don't know how much I'm going to be allowed to do for the patient."

"I've known Stepp for years, so you needn't explain him to me," Dr. Murdock assured her. "And if he gets in your way, tries to usurp your authority or your responsibility, give me a ring and I'll put him in his place."

Susan's eyes widened slightly, and Dr. Murdock chuckled.

"Oh, I don't mean physically," he answered the look in her eyes that she did not dare put into words. "Stepp could break me in two with one hand tied behind him. I meant I'll simply pull rank on him. After all, I *am* the attending physician, and I'll see that he respects my authority and yours."

"It's good to know somebody can handle him," Susan said. "Frankly he scares me just a little."

"Because he looks like Frankenstein's monster? He used to be a prizefighter, and his poor mug was battered to bits and his brain slightly addled before his manager dropped him. He went down into the gutter, out of which Mr. Cantrell lifted him and rehabilitated him. So it's natural that he just about worships Mr. Cantrell."

She had walked with him out of the house and to where his car, a sturdy, dependable-looking dark coupé, stood in the drive.

"Dr. Murdock, I know a nurse isn't supposed ever to question a doctor's orders or form of treatment," she began hesitantly. "But this drug you are planning to use—what's it like? I mean to use—"

"You've never heard of it, Miss Merrill; very few nurses or doctors in this country have," he explained carefully. "It's so new that it doesn't even have a name; only a number: EC 211. It's available in very small quantities from a firm of chemists in Hamburg, because even over there it is being used only experimentally on human beings. They've had some startling results and there have, of course, been many, many failures. But it is growing in importance and eventually it may even lick this endocarditis thing."

Susan drew a deep breath and told him quietly of the scene at the hospital when Gerard had quoted Tennyson to her. Dr. Murdock listened and nodded, and when she had finished he said quietly, "You've grown fond of him, haven't you?"

Despite her efforts, there was a film of tears in Susan's eyes, and her voice shook slightly.

"Who could help it?" she managed unsteadily.

Dr. Murdock's eyes were very gentle.

"If he were my own father, the father I never knew because I grew up in an orphanage, I couldn't love him more," he told her, and seemed unashamed that his own voice was not the crisply authoritative voice most doctors use. "No one who has ever come in contact with him could fail to care very deeply for him. And to be able to keep him with us for a few more years is something for which I would gladly give my own life. I'd trade mine for his, if I could, and feel I got all the best of the deal."

"Then this EC 211 you are planning to use is not dangerous?"

"Of course it is. Any purely experimental drug is. But if we didn't experiment with new drugs—" He broke off at the look in her eyes, and when he went on his voice had deepened. "I will tell you quite frankly, Miss Merrill: it *may* prolong his life. It definitely will not speed his departure. Is that what was worrying you?"

Susan answered huskily, "Yes, Doctor."

"Then you can put that worry away from you," Dr. Murdock assured her. "I wouldn't for the world risk anything that would shorten his stay here by so much as a day or an hour. What I want terribly to do is to give him more time than the hospital doctors think he has."

Susan said, with an effort to steady her voice, "I feel sure of that, Doctor."

His face was touched with a warm smile that suddenly made him look boyish and very attractive.

"That's good! I never like to work with a nurse who doesn't have confidence in me!"

Susan gave him a warm smile. "I don't imagine you've ever had to, Doctor," she answered.

"Well, thanks." He was obviously pleased at the compliment. "I'll see you tomorrow, then, as soon as my clinic patients have been attended to and I can be free for as long as need be."

He stepped into his car, and Susan handed him his small black bag. As he accepted it, he again gave her that oddly attractive smile and said quietly, "It's going to be good working with you, Nurse Merrill."

"I'm looking forward to it, too, Dr. Murdock," she assured him.

He studied her for a moment before he stared the car.

"I often wonder how much it might mean to a patient to know his doctor and his nurse are in perfect accord," he said.

Susan laughed. "I'm afraid most patients are chiefly concerned with how the nurse and doctor get along with their anxious relatives!"

"There's a point I'd rarely considered," he told her, and started the car, lifting his hand from the wheel for a little gesture of leave-taking.

As Susan turned to go back into the house, Maisie came to meet her.

"What did Dr. Murdock think, Miss Merrill?" she asked, and added swiftly, "I know I'm not supposed to ask. But we are all so worried, and we did so hope Dr. Murdock would find out the doctors at the hospital were wrong about him."

"He didn't, Maisie," Susan answered gently. "He confirmed the diagnosis, which was his to begin with. It seems he was the one who sent Mr. Cantrell to the hospital when the clinic couldn't provide facilities for caring for him."

Maisie's eager expression faded.

"Well, if Dr. Murdock doesn't think there's any hope, then there isn't." She accepted the fact without argument. "He's wonderful, Dr. Murdock is. Everybody likes him a lot."

Susan saw the touch of color in the girl's suntanned cheeks and said lightly. "A certain person named Maisie Blake, for instance? *You* think he's pretty wonderful, don't you?"

Maisie's eyes fell shyly away from Susan's as she answered awkwardly, "Now what good would it do *me* to think he was wonderful? He doesn't even know I'm alive. He treated me a year ago when I had strep throat, but nowadays when I see him on the street he can't even remember my name."

"Well, he probably has a large practice, hasn't he?"

"Oh, sure. The fishermen in the village and their families. And then he works two days a week at the hospital on the mainland. And there are summer visitors, and the rich and swanky ones that come to the Island and need doctoring," Maisie answered. "He works awfully hard, and people say that the light is on in his office until way after midnight nearly every night in the week. And he never takes a vacation, even for a weekend. Sometimes I wonder how he stands the pressure."

"I can answer that, Maisie. Because he loves medicine and is dedicated to his profession. You don't get tired when you're working at something you love very much, as I'm sure Dr. Murdock loves medicine."

Maisie studied her swiftly. "It's like that with you, isn't it, Miss Merrill?" she asked.

Susan smiled and nodded. "That's why I can understand how Dr. Murdock can stand the pressure of a large practice, Maisie."

"I hope I'll like teaching that much," Maisie answered, and there was a wistful note in her voice.

"Oh, are you going to be a teacher, Maisie? That's a wonderful profession."

Maisie answered, "I know it is, and I'm sure going to love it. But I have to work very hard to get a certificate. Right now, I have another year at Teachers' College, before I can hope to get a job."

As they walked into the house together, she added impulsively, "I used to think I wanted to be a nurse. But now I know I couldn't ever be, because the sight of blood makes me sick to my stomach."

Susan laughed. "Then you'd certainly never be a nurse, Maisie. I think you're very wise to be a teacher."

Maisie asked curiously, "Do you like being a nurse, Miss Merrill?"

"Well, of course I do, Maisie, or I'd never gone into training," Susan answered. "It's hard work; it's sometimes extremely unpleasant; there is very little glamour about it. But it's a very rewarding profession. To help people get well; to stand beside them when they are in pain or scared and helpless and do whatever you can to ease both their bodies and their minds—yes, Maisie, I love being a nurse."

As they reached the door of Gerard's room Susan added quietly, "Whatever profession you choose to follow, Maisie, whether it's nursing or teaching, you have to love it or you'll be no good at it. Always remember that, won't you?"

"Oh, yes, I will, Miss Merrill. I truly will! And thank you," said Maisie gratefully as she walked away down the corridor.

4

THE first forty-eight hours of the new treatment were anxious ones for Susan and Dr. Murdock, and for the Blakes and Stepp as well. They all went around on tiptoe, tense and anxiously waiting for some indications that the drug was going to be beneficial in its results.

On the third morning, when Gerard had no fever and his eyes were brighter, his pulse stronger, Susan and Dr. Murdock looked at each other with shining eyes in which their mutual delight was obvious.

"He's responding," said Dr. Murdock as though he had just witnessed a miracle.

Gerard looked up at them, and the impish twinkle beneath his bony brows was brighter than Susan had ever seen it.

"Don't stand there talking over me as if I couldn't hear you," he ordered them, and his voice was appreciably stronger. "I'm involved in this business, too, you know. Or had you forgotten that?"

"You're the core of this business, sir," Dr. Murdock assured him, exultation in his voice. "You're responding to the drug, and I'm delighted."

"Relieved, too, I dare say," Gerard observed with a slight trace of mockery.

"Well, of course, sir," Dr. Murdock agreed. "I told you in the very beginning the drug was purely experimental, and I couldn't guarantee it would have effect one way or the other. But you took a chance, and I'll always be grateful that you did, sir!"

Gerard studied him, the ghost of a smile touching his thin lips.

"I'm grateful you thought of it, my boy! Maybe the results of this will help others unlucky enough to get themselves into my condition," he said quietly.

When Susan followed Dr. Murdock out of the room, to receive final instructions for the care of the patient, Stepp followed her. After Dr. Murdock had gone, he asked Susan anxiously, "The chief's going to get well?"

"It's too soon yet to know, Stepp, but Dr. Murdock and I have high hopes for him," Susan answered.

"That's good news, after the hospital docs saying there wasn't any hope at all for him," Stepp answered, and with a deep breath put his powerful shoulders back and re-entered the sick room.

Susan had almost reached her own room when Maisie came hurrying to meet her, her face expressive of her deep anger and concern.

"Miss Merrill, there was a telegram just now, telephoned over from the mainland. We have to meet the family at the airport late this evening. The six o'clock flight from Atlanta."

"The family? But I didn't think Mr. Cantrell had a family," Susan protested.

"Oh, it's those two nephews and a niece I told you about," Maisie explained. "They've heard he is dying, and they're flocking around just like I told you they would. Oh, Miss Merrill, what are we going to do?"

Susan hesitated and then said quietly, "We'll have to welcome them, Maisie, and do the best we can. They mustn't be allowed to upset Mr. Cantrell, of course, but I don't see how anyone except Mr. Cantrell can refuse them permission to come."

"Oh, he wouldn't do that. He's too good and kind, and they *are* his sister's children, the only family he has," Maisie answered, and anger rode high in her eyes. "They are only coming because they've heard that he is dying and they want to be here for the reading of the will. They're his heirs, of course. Who else would be?"

"Maisie, that's a very unkind thing to say about them."

"Not half as unkind as they deserve. Miss Merrill, they are loathsome! You'll see! They'll turn the place upside down and make trouble for everybody! And if they get in to see Mr. Cantrell, it will be just too bad."

74

"Then we'll have to see that they don't," said Susan firmly.

Hope touched Maisie's eyes briefly.

"You'll keep them out, Miss Merrill?"

"Under doctor's orders, Maisie. You may be quite sure of that!" Susan promised her. "That's a big part of a nurse's job: to see that the patient is not disturbed by too much company or any that's unwelcome."

"Oh," said Maisie reluctantly, "I imagine he'll be glad to see them. He seems fond of them and always welcomes them, what few times they do come."

"Then maybe it might help him to see them?" suggested Susan.

"Well, maybe!" Obviously Maisie had grave doubts about that.

"Will they be here in time for dinner?"

"Oh, they'll expect dinner if they don't get here until midnight," Maisie answered grimly.

"You really do dislike them, don't you?" Susan asked.

"You will, too, as soon as you meet

them. You wait and see," Maisie said, and went back to the kitchen.

Susan hesitated for a moment, and then went into the library to the telephone and called Dr. Murdock. The moment she announced herself he asked sharply, "Is anything wrong?"

"Oh, no, not with the patient," Susan answered quickly. "It's just that some relatives of his are arriving on the six o'clock flight from Atlanta, and I wasn't sure whether I should prepare him for their arrival and let them see him when they arrive."

"The Barfords and Mrs. Gilbert, eh?" Dr. Murdock's voice was dry. "I was wondering when they'd show up. As soon as they got the news from the hospital, I suppose."

"Shall I tell him that they are coming?" asked Susan.

"Yes, you'd better. But they are not to be allowed to see him tonight. Tomorrow morning after I've seen him if he is still responding, the disease continuing its remission, we'll decide."

76

"Yes, Doctor," said Susan, and put down the receiver.

She crossed the wide reception hall to Gerard's door and entered.

He was laying propped against his pillows, looking out at the beloved view for which he had been so homesick during his stay in the hospital. He turned his head and smiled at her as she approached the bed.

"You're going to have some company," she told him gently.

His eyebrows went up slightly, and he waited.

"The family is arriving this evening," Susan finished.

For a moment his expression did not alter, and then he smiled.

"So they've found out, have they?" His voice was so low that Susan wasn't quite sure she had heard him correctly. He looked up at her and smiled. "My two nephews, David and Grady, and my niece Joyce. I suppose she will bring her little daughter with her. A lovely child, Susan, but I'd be much happier about her if she

77

was being brought up with a bit more discipline."

Susan smiled down at him. "Dr. Murdock doesn't want you to see them tonight. He wants you to wait until he has made his morning call and checked you again."

Gerard smiled back at her. "Then you'd better put a padlock and an armed guard on my door," he warned her.

"Oh, I'm sure they'll be very anxious to see you, but I'm also sure I can convince them that it's best they wait until morning," Susan told him.

"You'll have to be very convincing indeed, Susan my girl, to accomplish that!"

"Would you like to have them in for a few minutes, even against Dr. Murdock's orders?" Susan asked curiously.

"Of course not!" Gerard was quite firm about that. "I want to do exactly what Scott thinks is best. After all, he's trying to give me a few more years instead of a few more weeks. I owe it to him to co-operate to the fullest!"

"Fine," Susan approved the decision. "Then I'll meet them when they arrive and explain to them that the doctor doesn't want you to have any company until tomorrow."

"And Stepp will stand guard at the door, won't you, Stepp?"

Stepp's ugly face was set in a scowl that Susan felt could easily frighten even the most courageous. "You betcha, Chief! Nobody's coming in you don't want to come in. And that's for sure!"

But when, shortly before seven that night, Susan faced the newcomers in the library, she knew that Stepp had his work cut out for him. The two men were good-looking, excellently and expensively tailored, and the woman was lean, smart-looking, expensively and fashionably dressed.

"How is he?" It was the woman who spoke first.

"Oh, he's better," said Susan quickly.

The three exchanged swift, startled glances.

"Better?" Joyce Gilbert snapped as

though she could not believe her ears. "You mean he's *not* dying?"

The two young men made restive gestures toward her as though they would have silenced her.

"We hope not," said Susan quietly.

"Who's we?" snapped the younger of the two men.

"Dr. Murdock, Mr. Cantrell's doctor," Susan answered. "He is trying an experimental drug in the hope of affecting a remission in the disease."

"Experimental?" the oldest of the two men snapped. "By whose authority? I happen to know experimental drugs can't be administered without the consent of the patient's family."

"That's quite true, Mr. Barford," Susan answered coolly. "But Mr. Cantrell himself gave the permission and signed the necessary authorization paper."

"That's ridiculous," David Barford snapped at her. "A man in his condition, and this quack let him give such authority—"

"Dr. Murdock is not a quack, and Mr.

Cantrell was, and still is, in full possession of all his faculties and quite competent to make such a decision!" Susan flashed.

The three of them eyed her with cold inimical eyes, while the small child curled up in a chair and went to sleep.

"That's what *you* say!" David, the elder of the two Barford brothers, elected himself spokesman for his brother and his sister, and his voice had a biting quality. "I demand that we be allowed to see our uncle immediately, so we can judge for ourselves whether or not he is competent to make such a decision."

Susan stiffened beneath the whiplash of his voice and straightened her head high.

"I'm sorry, Mr. Barford, but that's against the doctor's orders."

"I'll bet it is!" Joyce spoke harshly, her voice quite as ugly as her brother's had been. "You and this quack doctor have had him all to yourselves here and have done anything you liked with him. So naturally, you are upset now that we have arrived to take care of him! I've met your kind of nurse before, miss! And I wouldn't trust you with a pet dog of mine."

Susan set her teeth hard to steady her voice so that she could speak firmly. "I'm sorry, Mrs. Gilbert. Maisie will show you to your rooms now, and I'm sure Elizabeth has dinner for you."

"We're going to see Uncle Gerry before we do anything else," snapped Joyce, and started across the hall, followed by her two brothers.

Stepp leaned against the closed door of Gerard's room, arms folded, watching them, waiting for them, his ugly jaw set and hard, his eyes dark with menace.

"Can't nobody see the chief tonight, folks," he drawled, and the Barfords stopped short before his look. "Doctor's orders."

"This is ridiculous!" blazed Joyce furiously.

"The chief's a sick man, ma'am, and can't be disturbed by folks barging in on him just as he gets to sleep," Stepp insisted, and seemed almost bland.

"We're his family," David protested.

Stepp eyed him with a cold look.

"Right funny you didn't think of that a long time ago when the chief was feelin' good and would have been proud to see you," he suggested.

"How dare you criticize us?" snapped David.

Stepp's eyebrows went up slightly.

"Was I criticizing you, Mr. Barford? I was just mentioning facts, is all." Stepp's tone was as close to a purr as he could make it, and even that was touched with contempt.

Elizabeth came into view, and Susan was quite sure she had been standing in the shadows near the kitchen wing overhearing the whole scene. But she came forward with a bland, expressionless face, and her voice was quiet.

"I've spread supper for you folks in the dining room," she said. "Sandy's putting your luggage in your rooms. I reckon you're pretty tired and you'd like a good night's rest before you visit the chief."

For a moment the three stood irresolute, exchanging glances that Susan could interpret only too well. However, one glance at Stepp seemed to make up their minds, and with ill grace they followed Elizabeth to the dining room.

The child stirred, awoke, found the room empty and gave vent to an outraged cry. Susan hurried into the library and knelt beside her, to put her arms about the child. But the latter drew back a small clenched fist and struck her with surprising strength on the jaw.

"Why, baby!" Susan gasped, and sat back on her heels, staring at the child in amazement. "I was only going to take you to your mother and get you some supper."

"I don't want my mother! I want Ellen!" wailed the child, and burst into tears.

Joyce came hurrying into the room, angry and impatient.

"For heaven's sake, you little brat, stop that row!" she snapped, and caught the child by the shoulders and shook her hard. "Now come on and have some supper and go to bed."

84

"I want Ellen!" screamed the child.

Joyce shook her again.

"Ellen's not here and you darned well know it! Now be quiet, or I'll spank you!" she snapped.

The child looked up at her uncertainly, her rosebud mouth opened for a howl. But as she met her mother's cold, angry eyes she gulped back the howl and, to Susan's astonishment, slid docilely off the chair and walked beside her mother out of the room.

Susan went back to the door, where Stepp still stood guard, and he grinned at her.

"I heard a fellow say once that there's two schools of thought about raising kids," he volunteered. "One was to bring 'em up the way they ought to be; and the other was just to let the FBI handle it later on. From what I've seen of *that* one, it ain't hard to decide which school her mother is following."

"But, Stepp, she's only a baby, and a beautiful child!" protested Susan.

85

Stepp lifted his massive shoulders in a gesture that was an attempt at a shrug.

"She's three years old and a little hellion," he countered. "But when you think about how she's being raised, who can wonder? That mother of hers—" His lip curled in disgust, and Susan could only stare at him in shocked surprise.

"Sure, Miss Merrill, I know you think I ought to be horse-whipped for speaking like that about the chief's folks. And if they was the right kind of folks, and cared about him instead of his money, I'd be the first one to praise 'em to the skies. But when I think of what they really are —no, ma'am, I don't want any part of them, not ever no time."

Susan said hesitantly, "Well, of course I don't know them."

"And you're lucky, miss," Stepp assured her firmly. "I just wish you could keep it like that. But they're here, and you're going to be tripping over them everywhere you turn. Just watch your step, miss, and don't let 'em run over you. They will, if you show the slightest sign of weakness! Believe me, the Blakes and me *know* 'em and wish we didn't.''

Susan asked, "Is Mr. Cantrell asleep?"

"Not him, miss. You want to see him?" Stepp stood aside and opened the door, and Susan stepped inside the room. Stepp immediately shut the door and once more put himself on guard.

Gerard lay against his pillows watching her, and she was delighted at the look of wry amusement in his eyes.

"Now that you've met my loving family, Susan, what do you think of them?" There was mockery in his voice and in his eyes.

"That's an unfair question," Susan countered. "I've only just met them. They are very eager to see you, but Dr. Murdock preferred to have them wait until after he makes his morning visit and checks on your condition."

"Bless Dr. Murdock!" said Gerard dryly.

Susan gave him a sedative and sat beside him until he slept before she left the room. She nodded to Stepp as she went on back to her own quarters.

She opened the door and then stood, wide-eyed, for Joyce was busily unpacking her luggage, and Susan's belongings were piled in an untidy heap at the foot of the bed.

Joyce flung her a hostile glance.

"This is always my room when I'm at the Cedars," she said curtly. "I've told the Blake woman to have your things transferred to the room they wanted to put me in: a maid's room across the corridor and at the end. It is a suitable room for an employee; hardly the room to be given to a member of the family."

She went on unpacking, and Susan leaned against the door frame and watched her.

"Aren't you being pretty high-handed?" she asked quietly.

Joyce straightened from her task of piling cobwebby underthings in the bureau drawer from which she had just removed Susan's much more utilitarian garb.

"My dear young woman," she said haughtily, "you should be occupying the room adjoining my uncle's; not here clear across the house from him. And as for being high-handed, naturally, being a member of the family, I wanted my own room. I'm tired and I want to get some sleep. If you'll get out and take your things with you, I'll be able to get to bed."

For a moment Susan hesitated. And then, with a slight shrug, she picked up an armful of her belongings and went out of the room, meeting Maisie in the hall.

"You're going to let her get away with it?" Maisie asked, obviously disappointed.

"It hardly seems worth a fuss, Maisie!" Susan answered. "I have an idea there's going to be a lot to fuss about in the next few days, so why start off by refusing to surrender what she claims is the room she always occupies when she is here? Will you help me by getting the rest of my things and then show me this room I'm supposed to use?"

"The chief won't like this," said Maisie grimly. "Not one single little bit he won't!"

"There's no reason he should know, Maisie," Susan soothed her. "After all, I'm more accustomed to sharing a cubbyhole in a dormitory with another nurse than to having a large, luxurious room like that all to myself. So let's get going, shall we?"

"Well, sure, if that's the way you want it," said Maisie unhappily, and went back into the room, scooped the balance of Susan's possessions up in her arms and led the way down the hall and across to an open door.

Susan looked about her. The room was small but well furnished, and there was a small bath. Maisie watched her anxiously.

"You don't mind being in here?" Maisie asked.

"Why should I?" Susan was busily hanging her uniforms tidily in the closet.

"It's a very nice room, and I'm sure the view will be very good when it's daylight and I can see it. No, Maisie, I don't mind a bit."

Maisie was putting things away in the drawers of the big chifforobe and spoke over her shoulder.

"Well, I still think she had her nerve throwing you out of the room the chief wanted you to have," she said frankly.

"What about the two men? Could you find room for them?"

"Oh, sure, there's plenty of room, except they didn't like having to room together. There's a huge room with twin beds and a bath and a dressing room, but they felt each should have had one of their own." Maisie straightened and faced Susan, her fists planted on her hips in a stance that was so like her mother that Susan's eyes twinkled. "This is what always happens when they come down here. But praises be, it's never more than once a year or once in two years!"

"Then we'll make the best of it, won't we?" suggested Susan.

"If you say so," Maisie answered
without conviction, and went back to
helping Susan dispose of her possessions
in the closet and the chifforobe.

5

IN the morning when Susan went into Gerard's room, he was bathed, shaved and in fresh pajamas. Stepp had sternly refused from the first to let Susan attend to these duties, despite her insistence that as Gerard's nurse it was part of her job.

Gerard smiled at her warmly, and her fingers on his pulse told her that he was stronger. There was no fever. Highly elated, she beamed down at him.

"You're doing just fine!" she told him happily.

"Think I'll make those extra years?"

"Well, of course you will. Dr. Murdock and I wouldn't hear of anything else."

Gerard asked gently, "Does my family know that I have been given a reprieve?"

"Yes, and they are delighted," Susan

assured him firmly. And forced herself to meet his eyes.

"You are lying in your teeth, Susie m'girl," Gerard told her flatly. "I'll bet they were shocked to the socks when they found they'd made a trip down here for nothing, after they had come with every assurance they would be here in time for the funeral! And now you and Scott have fooled them! They won't love you for that, Susie! Believe me they won't!"

"Please don't talk like that, Mr. Cantrell!" Susan made no effort to conceal her distress, and Gerard's smile, though faint, was comforting.

"Then I won't, Susie."

Stepp said suddenly, "Here's Dr. Murdock," and swung the door open for him.

Scott Murdock thanked him, smiled a good morning to Susan and turned swiftly to the patient. Susan saw the anxiety in his eyes as he began his examination. But by the time he had finished it, his anxiety had melted beneath a delight that Susan found touching.

Gerard asked, "Think I'll make it, Scott?"

"You'll make it, sir. You'll make it." Though Dr. Murdock's voice was quiet, its tone made the words sound like a shout of triumph.

"That's good, for both of us," said Gerard. He added as Dr. Murdock's brows went up slightly, "For me, for so many reasons they need not be mentioned. For you, because if you've found something that will slow this type of endocarditis, you'll be famous."

"I'll be lucky," Dr. Murdock assured him gravely. "The fame is not half as important as seeing you looking so hale and hearty this morning. There's nothing that could make me happier."

Before Gerard could answer that there was the sound of voices outside and a peremptory rap on the door. Joyce's voice was raised in a bitter argument with Stepp, who stood stolidly on guard.

Dr. Murdock glanced at Susan and then at Gerard, who cocked an eyebrow at him and said resignedly, "You may as well let them in. There'll be no peace in the house until you do."

Susan accepted Dr. Murdock's nod as permission and walked to the door, opening it behind Stepp's solid back that was barring the three relatives.

"It's all right, Stepp," she told him in the even, all but expressionless tone of her profession. "Dr. Murdock says they may have five minutes with the patient."

"I must say, after we've traveled all the way down here from New York, that's darned big of him," snapped David Barford, and led the way into the room, the other two trooping behind him.

Gerard lay against his pillows, watching them, an inscrutable look in his eyes.

"Well, Uncle Gerry, it's harder to get in to see you than it is to see the President," said David, and made an effort to lighten his tone with a surface gaiety that would conceal his resentment.

"We came last night," said Joyce, slim and smart in beige tapered pants and a striped shirt. "But this nurse creature refused to let us see you! I think you

96

should fire her, Uncle. Why, she had my room and was making herself very much at home in it."

"And why not?" asked Gerard, and there was a sting in his voice. "I arranged for her to have that room, since it is so seldom occupied."

"Well, it is now. I didn't lose any time rooting her out, I can tell you!" said Joyce, and added, her eyes on his face, "You're looking wonderful, Uncle. I'm so pleased."

"Are you?" asked Gerard.

Color crept up beneath the too heavy make-up on Joyce's lean face, and her head tilted at a defiant angle.

"Well, of course I am, Uncle. They gave us such a terrible story at the hospital that the boys and I rushed right down on a chartered plane, so that we could be here last night. And then this woman wouldn't let us see you," Joyce complained.

"At my orders, Mrs.—" Dr. Murdock hesitated, unsure of her name. Her glance flicked him and dismissed him.

"I'm Mrs. Gilbert, Uncle Gerard's only niece," she told him curtly. "And these are my brothers, David and Grady Barford."

They nodded. Nobody offered to shake hands. To Susan, there was an atmosphere of such cold hostility in the room that she could not control a slight shiver as she waited for Gerard's next move.

"Better take them into the library, Scott, and explain to them what you are doing for me and why I hope to beat the prognosis by at least a few years," he suggested.

"A few *years?*" Joyce gasped, too shocked to control her expression of dismay and protest.

The two young men flung angry glances at her as they moved toward the door, but Gerard addressed Joyce quietly. "With the experimental drug Scott is using, he thinks we may be able to make it a few years instead of a few weeks. I know you will all be overjoyed to hear that."

There was a thin edge of contempt and sarcastic amusement in his voice. But

Joyce stammered something about being overjoyed, and Dr. Murdock managed to get them out of the room.

"You'd better go along, too, Susan, to back Scott up. He'll need help. Stepp will be here with me," said Gerard, and now there was a deep, sick weariness in his eyes that made Susan want to cry. "Run along, Susan. I'll be quite all right."

Susan set her teeth hard and walked out of the room and to the library, where Dr. Murdock was explaining to the three relatives just what he was trying to accomplish in the treatment of a disease from which recovery was extremely rare.

The three of them were listening, scowling and angry. When Dr. Murdock paused for breath David Barford asked sharply, "Are you trying to tell me that he's *not* going to die?"

"The hospital said two or three weeks at best," Joyce added.

Dr. Murdock glanced around at the three scowling, intent faces and then at Susan, who stood unobtrusively beside the door.

"I have every hope that with the treatment he's getting now, we can extend that to a year, perhaps two or even more—" Dr. Murdock began. But a mingled murmur of fury stopped him.

David said sharply to them, "Quiet, you two!" and turned to Dr. Murdock. "You say this drug you're using on him is purely experimental? You have no idea what it will do, one way or another?"

"I have a very good idea," Dr. Murdock insisted. "I am quite hopeful that it will slow the disease, cause a remission—"

"But not a complete cure?" David insisted.

"At his age, that would be an impossible hope. The heart is seriously damaged, even without this subacute bacterial infection," Dr. Murdock began defensively.

"But still you're making a guinea pig out of him; using a drug that has never before been tried on a human being?" David demanded.

"That's not true. It's been used abroad."

"I mean here in this country."

"There have been some cases in which it has been used."

"With what results?"

"Some good, some not so good."

"Then we, his family, forbid you to go on with this treatment," David said sharply, and the others added their voices to that.

Susan all but held her breath. But Scott Murdock merely stood there, his hands in his pockets, leaned against the edge of a big heavy table and studied them slowly, one after the other.

"I'm afraid your objection to the treatment comes a bit late," he said coolly. "The patient himself gave me permission some days ago and has been showing marked improvement ever since."

There was an angry silence before he turned to the door, smiled at Susan and said, "We'll continue the treatment as before, Nurse."

"Yes, Doctor," said Susan demurely, and walked with him out of the house and to his car.

She shivered in the warm spring sun, and Dr. Murdock glanced down at her, noting the shiver, his eyes bleak.

"Nice people," he commented dryly. "I'm sure you got the same impression I did about them?"

Susan looked up at him, afraid to put the question.

"That they don't want him to react to the drug and have a few more years," said Dr. Murdock grimly. "They hoped to get here just in time for the funeral and the reading of the will, before they rushed back to their own lives."

"It sounds horrible when you put it in words, doesn't it?" Susan asked huskily.

"It does. And it is horrible," Dr. Murdock answered, and for a moment he studied her with a smile that warmed as he took in the picture she made in the spring sunshine in her crisp uniform. "Don't let it get you down, Susan. You've probably met people like these before. They are not nearly so rare as one might like to believe. But we are going to fight them, Susan, to a standstill!"

"We are?" asked Susan.

"We are indeed," said Dr. Murdock firmly. "You are in complete authority to keep them out of his room. Doctor's orders, and Stepp will see to it that your orders are obeyed."

Susan drew a deep breath and lifted her head.

"Stepp and I will protect him, Doctor, I promise," she said quietly.

"Sure you will," said Dr. Murdock. Suddenly it was as though he were really seeing her for the first time as he studied her. "Hi, the chief, as Stepp calls him, really hit it lucky, getting a pretty young thing like you for his nurse. You really are beautiful, Susan; did you know that?"

Susan's face warmed even as she laughed. "Are you trying to build up my morale, Doctor?"

"Well, no. I don't really think it needs it." Dr. Murdock seemed to consider the matter thoughtfully. "I suppose I've just been too absorbed in the case to notice what a pretty nurse I'm working with.

Come to think of it, the chief and I are both very lucky indeed."

"Why, thank you, Doctor," she mocked him lightly.

"One of these days, when the invasion has moved out, you must give me a chance to become better acquainted, off duty. Have dinner with me, and we'll talk about other things than patients and drugs and treatment."

"Such as what, Doctor?" she dared impishly.

"Oh, I'll think of something when the time comes," he promised her, and saw the color deepen in her cheeks, before he added briskly, "If you have any trouble with the invaders, don't hesitate to give me a ring; and I'll gallop to the rescue, complete with Marines and the county sheriff, if it seems advisable."

"Thank you, Doctor," said Susan, and managed a laugh. "I don't really think it will come to that. I imagine once they are convinced he isn't at death's door, they'll go back where they came from."

"Which couldn't be too soon for either of us, could it?"

"It really couldn't, Doctor," Susan agreed with him.

He got into his car, gave a little gesture of farewell, and the car went rolling down the drive.

Susan stood watching it for a moment. She liked this young doctor enormously and felt herself to be very lucky that she had this chance to work with him.

A small smile curled her mouth as she stood there on the terrace, her bemused eyes on the drive where Dr. Murdock's car had vanished.

Whom do you think you are kidding? a small voice inside of her mocked. You know darned well you like him for himself, as well as for his ability as a doctor. Remember, Maisie told you practically the entire village, especially the feminine section of it, is mad about him. So don't go trying to tell *me* you find him attractive just because he's a fine doctor.

6

BEFORE she took her off-duty hours that afternoon, Susan assured herself that everything was in order in the sick room. Gerard was sleeping peacefully and Stepp was on guard, so she had no compunctions about leaving them.

From the library she could hear the murmur of voices and knew that the "family" was holding a conclave. She slipped quietly back to her own room and got into her bathing suit, which Gerard had insisted she bring with her. Over it she belted a knee-length terry-cloth robe, thrust her feet into straw beach slippers, and went through the kitchen towards the back terrace.

Elizabeth and Maisie were on the terrace shelling peas for dinner, and as she appeared, Elizabeth nodded approval.

"Now, that's right, Miss Susan. You go get a nice swim. Maisie says the water's like warm milk and the wind's not a bit cold."

Susan laughed. "I'm afraid it will be a wade, not a swim, Mrs. Blake. I can't swim."

Elizabeth's sandy eyebrows went up in shocked surprise.

"Why, now, is that a fact?" she marveled. "Why, it's easy as anything. You want Maisie to teach you?"

Maisie laughed. "Now, Mom, what woman wants another woman to teach her to swim? That's a man's job!"

Elizabeth grinned at her. "Well, your father never learned to swim a stroke, and I wouldn't know about Stepp. Anyway, he's on duty with the chief."

Susan laughed. "Would I shock you both if I admitted frankly that I don't want to learn to swim? The thought terrifies me. I'm a devout coward. I'll take my water sports in the bathtub. I just wanted to go for a walk on the beach and maybe dabble a toe or two in the tide. I won't be long."

"You be gone as long as you like, honey. We'll hold the fort," Elizabeth called after her, and Susan flung up a hand in gay response as she went down the steep slope, and found the stone steps set into each terrace that led to the water-line.

She waded out ankle-deep, and the swirling of the milk-warm water about her legs was very soothing. She ventured further, but when the next wave splashed her above the knees, she panicked and turned back, hurrying to escape the clutch of the wave, that now seemed like unfriendly fingers reaching for her.

She dropped down on the beach and relaxed contentedly. Watching the sandpipers that scuttled just above the line of each succeeding breaker, always managing to sidestep just in time to escape being caught. Overhead the sky was a blue so deep, so sun-drenched that the eyes ached with looking at it. A flight of pelicans, a dozen or more in the line, floated across the blue sky, and Susan watched them, entranced by their perfect co-ordination. They flew in a straight line, one behind the other, with exactly the same space between each two. The leader set the pace. Now and then he would raise and lower his wings; number two would follow suit; then number three and so on down the line. They were like a drill team, flying in perfect rhythm, and Susan had the crazy feeling that she could hear music to which they were performing.

Suddenly the leader folded his wings and plummeted straight to the sea and vanished beneath it. A moment later he rose, and the sunlight silvered the fish he held in his beak. Instantly behind him, one after another, the others dived.

Susan was so absorbed in watching them that she was not aware of Grady Barford's presence until he spoke above her head and she looked up at him, startled.

"Amusing critters, aren't they?" said Grady, nodding toward the pelicans. "May I join you?"

He was in swimming trunks, a robe tossed carelessly over his shoulders, and he did not wait for her permission before he dropped down beside her, asking the inevitable question, "How's the water?"

Susan laughed. "Well, I only went in knee-deep, but it was quite warm and very nice."

He raised his eyebrows. "You didn't swim?"

"I can't swim," Susan confessed, and added, "Don't hesitate to look shocked. Mrs. Blake and Maisie were."

"Who's Mrs. Blake?"

"The housekeeper."

"Oh, her," Grady dismissed Mrs. Blake as though surprised that Susan should even have mentioned her. "I don't imagine it would take much to shock the Great Stone Face. That's what Joyce calls her, and I must say the name fits. But let's not talk about her. Let's talk about us. Do you like being a nurse?"

"Well, of course, or I wouldn't be one."

"As simple as that, eh? You're lucky:

to be able to be what you want to be," he answered. He added, as his eyes took her in from the top of her bronze-gold head to the tips of her toes in the beach sandals, "I'd like very much to dress you."

Susan gasped and her eyes flew wide. Grady laughed.

"Oh, don't be shocked. I'm not making a pass. I was just thinking what a wonderful model you'd make for my shop. What a delight it would be to design things for you. Your coloring is superb! Be careful not to get too tanned, won't you? You're perfect just as you are."

Susan blinked. "You lost me somewhere," she confessed. "I haven't the ghost of an idea what you're talking about."

"Haven't you? I'm talking about trying to persuade you to model for me when I open my House of Barford." Obviously, to him, that was all the explanation required.

"The House of Barford? It sounds

quite exciting," she murmured politely, still completely at a loss to know what he was talking about.

"Oh, didn't Uncle tell you? I'm the family black sheep. I design women's clothes. And I'm very good at it," he told her cheerfully. "I did the costumes for a couple of off-Broadway shows. The shows were not sensationally successful, but the costumes received fine reviews. I've had some fairly exciting offers from other fashion houses, but I'm waiting until I can have my own place. Why should I give my best designs to someone who will only pay me a salary, even if it is a fancy one, when the same designs could be building a reputation for the House of Barford?"

Susan nodded. "That makes good sense," she replied politely.

"With you as a model, I feel I could do something that would arouse instant attention," he told her.

"That's crazy, Mr. Barford."

"Call me Grady, Susan."

"Well, Grady or Mr. Barford, the idea is still crazy!"

"Why?"

"Why? Well, because I'm a nurse."

"My dear girl, as my top model you'd make more money in a week than a nurse makes in a month or two. Besides which, you'd be a celebrity. Of course you'd have to take some training. One doesn't become a top fashion model just because one has superb coloring and fine bones and a stunning figure. It takes quite a bit more than that," he assured her.

"I'm sure it does. But I took four years training to become a nurse, and it's work that I love."

He stared at her as though she had just said a shocking thing.

"You're kidding!" he protested. "Nobody could love hanging around sick people and doing messy jobs in operating rooms and working long hours and being shockingly underpaid. You'll love being a model and wearing gorgeous clothes, because the clothes I'll design for you *will* be gorgeous ones; and being seen in all

the right places by the right people—"
He broke off because she was frankly
laughing at him. "What's so funny?"

"You are, Mr. Barford—oh, all right,
Grady then—" she said, "thinking you
could talk me out of my love for nursing.
Anyway I have no qualification for model-
ing even if I had any desire to model
which, believe me, I don't."

Grady Barford studied her, scowling a
little as though she were a creature whose
like he had never encountered before.

"The qualifications you have are exactly
what I'd hoped but never expected to
find," he assured her a trifle stiffly. "The
coloring, the bone structure, the figure.
Knowing how to walk, how to sit, how
best to show a gown—all that is a matter
of training. And an intelligent girl like
you—"

"Is much too intelligent, Grady, to give
up a profession she loves, and for which
she is said to possess some skill by doctors
with whom she has worked, to embark on
a career in a field of which she knows
absolutely nothing and in which she

hasn't the faintest interest. But thanks for the compliment, anyway."

"My privilege." He grinned ruefully at her. "I admit that when I first set eyes on you, I was intrigued, because, as I said, I'd hoped to find a girl like you but hadn't really expected to. I have been thinking ever since I first saw you that if I could have you as my top model, when I open the House of Barford, half my battle to get established would be won."

"That's very flattering but it's quite out of the question," Susan answered, and went on politely, "When are you opening your new fashion house?"

Grady met her eyes squarely, and there was cynicism in them.

"There's a little problem of money involved," he admitted, "rather a lot of money. You don't set up a place like that on nickels and dimes. I have an option on a spot that will be perfect, provided I can get the money for the purchase price before my option expires. I raked and scraped, begged and borrowed and would have stolen if I'd had to—only I didn't know anybody careless enough with money to make it worthwhile—all to get the money to buy the option. And if it is not taken up, if it's allowed to expire, I'll lose everything I put into the option and be in debt up to here. And that's no way to set up a business, especially as chancy a one as the fashion business."

Susan said quietly, "So you came down here to borrow the money from Mr. Cantrell to buy your shop."

Grady shot her a narrow-eyed glance, and his smile was thin and mirthless.

"That proves how little you know my uncle, if you think he'd give or lend me five cents for a business which he regards with complete scorn," he told her.

Susan sat very still, while the full impact of the situation struck her. Grady, like David and Joyce, had come there expecting to find Gerard either dead or dying and anticipating that the will would divide his estate into three equal parts.

She drew a hard breath and clenched her hands in the pockets of her robe. She lifted her chin and turned her head, meeting Grady's eyes and making no effort to hide the cold contempt that bubbled up within her.

Grady saw the look, understood it, and gestured with a casual movement of a very well-kept hand.

"After all, the money will all be ours eventually, so I can't see anything wrong in our coming here to protect our interests, can you?" he argued reasonably. "I want this fashion business, Susan. I've never wanted anything so much in my life. I've worked hard, studied, planned, sat up all night creating new designs; and now I'm ready! And I want to get started before that option expires."

Susan said stiffly, "Surely if you asked your uncle, explained to him—"

"You think I haven't?" Grady's jaw was set and hard, his eyes bleak.

"What happened?"

"Nothing! He was perfectly willing to finance me in any other business, just as he financed Dave through law school and got him set with one of the finest legal firms in New York. But when I told him what I wanted to do, he was disgusted. Refused to have any part in letting me make a fool of myself, was the way he expressed it. He felt that designing clothes for women was a sissy business, unworthy of his nephew, although most of the greatest, most famous designers in the world are men! No, Susan, I have no hope of getting any help from him."

Susan asked uneasily, "Then what *will* you do?"

Grady met her eyes.

"Wait," he said quietly.

And then he rose to his feet and went swinging off down the beach and dropped his robe. He sprang into a huge breaker that was rolling in toward the beach and went swimming strongly out into the ultra-blue ocean.

Susan sat very still for a long, stunned moment. "Wait!" he had said. She knew that he had meant wait until Gerard was dead. And the thought sent a cold chill through her that made her shiver, though the sun was warm overhead and the light salt-tangy breeze was as mild as a zephyr.

Grady came striding back up the beach, picked up his beach towel and began drying himself briskly as he looked down at her.

"Of course you aren't going to repeat anything I've said to my uncle?" His tone made it a statement rather than a question.

"Of course not, even though, if he were stronger, I'd feel I should," she admitted impulsively, making no effort to disguise her disgust.

Grady dropped to one knee beside her and studied her with a sharp steady scrutiny that made her heart slow a little.

"This experiment you and that hayseed doc are trying on Uncle isn't going to be successful, of course?"

Susan stood up with effortless and unconscious grace, whipped up her beach towel and stood before him, her head erect and her eyes cold.

"That's something I can't discuss with you," she told him curtly.

His hand shot out and caught her arm. "You're going to answer my question before you leave this beach! Is it?"

Susan said curtly, "The prospects are good. He is responding to the drug. There is a slight but definite remission in his disease. There is, of course, still grave danger. But Dr. Murdock feels his chances are more than fair.

"For how long?"

"A few years."

"A few *years*?" Grady looked as though he had been kicked in the stomach.

"Yes," said Susan coolly. "The hospital felt, when he came home, that the best he could hope for was a few weeks, perhaps no more than three or four. But with the drug Dr. Murdock is using, we hope that he will have a few years longer."

She turned and walked back up the beach and on to the house without looking back.

Grady watched her go, his face black with helpless fury, before he dropped down on the beach, drew up his knees, rested his crossed arms across them and lowered his head to rest against his arms.

Susan reached the house and hurried to her own room. She felt cold as though the day had suddenly turned chilly. She got out of her bathing suit, showered and put on a fresh uniform, her mind working busily. By the time she had reached the sick room and Stepp had admitted her, she knew that she had to see Dr. Murdock and tell him about that scene on the beach. They were drawn up together against the invaders, as Dr. Murdock had expressed it. And between them they must somehow go on protecting the patient. That sounded, she warned herself even as the thought crossed her mind, very melodramatic; yet she knew that it was quite true.

Gerard was still sleeping peacefully. Stepp stared at Susan as she went swiftly to the bed and carefully checked the patient's pulse and respiration before she turned to him and motioned him toward the room that Stepp occupied. There, in the doorway, out of hearing of the sleeping man, she said softly, "Stepp, I have to talk to Dr. Murdock."

"Well, sure, miss. He'll be here before long."

"I want to talk to him away from the house."

Stepp stiffened, and his eyes went cold and hard.

"Something's up, miss?" he demanded and his voice was a low-pitched growl.

"I don't know, Stepp. I'm all mixed up. But there is something I think Dr. Murdock should know, and I want to be sure that we are not overheard," Susan told him, and added hastily, "Oh, I know I sound melodramatic and maybe silly; but, Stepp, don't leave him alone one single minute! And don't let anyone in here until I get back."

Stepp said grimly, "Don't fret, miss. Nobody but you and the Doc will get in here. That's for sure!"

"Good, Stepp! I know I can count on you," said Susan, and there was deep relief in her voice. "I won't be any longer than I can help."

"You be gone as long as you like, miss. I'll take care of the chief!" said Stepp in a voice that told her an army with guns wouldn't be allowed in the room as long as Stepp was on guard.

Susan hurried into the kitchen, where Elizabeth and Maisie were busy with dinner preparations, and asked, "Do you suppose Sandy would mind driving me to the village? I have some things to do."

Elizabeth looked at her, startled.

"Sakes, no, Miss Merrill. Sandy'd be glad to do anything he can for you. Maisie, you call him and tell him Miss Merrill needs him," ordered Elizabeth, and Maisie hurried out. "What's wrong, Miss Merrill?" Elizabeth asked quietly when Maisie had gone.

Susan hesitated and then said awkwardly, "Why, nothing, really. I'm just—well, a bit jittery, I suppose, and I wanted a conference with Dr. Murdock where I was quite sure there would be no one to overhear."

Elizabeth nodded in complete understanding.

"Seems a right sensible idea to me, miss," she answered softly.

"Dad's ready, Miss Merrill." Maisie appeared at the kitchen door, and Susan thanked her and hurried out into the late afternoon sunshine.

7

DR. MURDOCK'S clinic was housed in what had once been a summer resident's tabby-brick cottage. There was a neat small lawn, flower-bordered, behind a low picket fence, and an open door with an "Office" sign.

Susan turned to Sandy as she got out of the station wagon.

"You needn't wait, Sandy. I'll ride back with Dr. Murdock, and I may have to wait until he's finished his office hours."

"Sure, miss," said Sandy, and eyed her curiously as she went up the walk, the ocean wind tugging at her crisply starched skirts and blowing her hair beneath the cherished small cap.

She entered the pleasant, simply furnished office and saw that there were two patients waiting: a middle-aged woman who sat slumped in an attitude of bitter resignation and a younger woman with a small child on her lap. They watched Susan as she came in. As she sat down the younger woman leaned toward her.

"You're a nurse, aren't you, miss?" she asked. "Is Doc going to have a nurse here at the clinic?"

"No, I'm the nurse at the Cedars. My patient is Mr. Cantrell, and Dr. Murdock is treating him," answered Susan courteously. "What a handsome little boy!"

"Why, thank you. He's a handful, though, I can tell you," said his proud mother. Just then the door to the treatment room opened and Dr. Murdock ushered out a man who was hobbling on crutches, one foot wearing an enormous dressing and held very high above the floor.

"You keep off that foot now, Andy, and take care of yourself," Dr. Murdock was saying as the door opened.

The resigned-looking, middle-aged

woman stood up, and her voice was dry, rasping with contempt.

"Oh, don't worry none about him being too active, Doc. He's allus tickled to death to have some excuse not to stir a finger or move out of his chair," she whined.

"Now, Mamie—" the man murmured, glancing unhappily at the others in the room. "Women, Doc! You can't live with 'em and you can't live without 'em, seems like."

"And a nice kettle o' fish you men-folks would be in if it wasn't for us women-folks," sniffed the woman, and all but pushed him out of the room. "Man your age stepping on a rusty nail! That's for kids, not growed up men."

Dr. Murdock turned and his eyes fell on Susan.

"Why, Susan, is something wrong at the Cedars?" he asked, and her face colored slightly at the look of pleasure in his eyes as he saw her.

"I had some shopping to do in the village," Susan managed, conscious of the intensely interested eyes and ears of the woman with the child on her lap, and improvising swiftly. "I didn't want to keep Sandy waiting, so I thought I'd hitch a ride back to the Cedars with you, if you don't mind."

"Well, of course I don't mind. I'm delighted!" Dr. Murdock assured her, and turned to the waiting woman and the child. "And now, Mrs. Sanders, let's see how our boy is getting along."

Susan was beginning to feel a bit silly by the time the woman and child emerged from the treatment room and were given a prescription to be filled at the village pharmacy. When Dr. Murdock came over to her she looked up at him and said miserably, "I'm beginning to feel like a fool, Doctor."

Dr. Murdock shook his head. "That's something you could never be, Susan. Now tell me all about it."

Swiftly and as briefly as she could she repeated to him the scene on the beach with Grady Barford. And as she talked Dr. Murdock's scowl deepened. When she had finished he studied her silently for a moment.

"So you see, Doctor," she stammered miserably, "I *am* being a fool to rush down here like this and tell you about it. But, Doctor, I'm scared!"

Tears were slipping uncontrollably down her cheeks, and it seemed the most natural thing in the world that he should reach out to her and draw her into his arms, holding her comfortably while she wept. Finally shame and embarrassment overwhelmed her and she drew herself free of him and looked up at him, scarcely able to meet his eyes.

"That was most unprofessional of me, Doctor," she said in apology. "I know nurses don't cry. But if you could have seen his face when I told him that you hoped Mr. Cantrell would have a few more years, instead of the weeks the hospital had promised—" She shivered and added impulsively, "He looked dangerous!"

"Oh, he did, did he? Well, now, we'll see about that."

Susan asked uneasily, "You don't think I'm being melodramatic?"

"Of course not. I think you're being very professional in wanting to protect your patient, and it's nonsense that nurses don't cry. They wouldn't be human if they didn't at times, and who'd want a nurse so callous that she couldn't weep now and then?"

"You're very kind, Doctor," she stammered gratefully.

He smiled slightly, though the smile did little to relieve the anxious look in his eyes.

"In that case, do you suppose you and I could be friends, Susan?"

Wide-eyed, she replied "Why, of course, Doctor. I thought we were!"

"Then do you suppose you could possibly call me Scott, instead of Doctor?"

In spite of her uneasiness and her confusion, Susan managed a demure, "Would that be professional, Doctor?"

He grinned, and she sensed that he was trying to ease her out of the mood that had brought her to tears.

"It might be fun," he pointed out. "Just between friends, of course."

He got up then and strode about the office, hands sunk deeply in the pockets of his white jacket, his brows drawn together in a worried scowl. At last he stopped and stood still in front of her.

"Susan, is it your impression that if this Barford fellow got the chance, he might do something to injure Mr. Cantrell?"

"If you mean," said Susan, her voice low and not quite steady, "do I think he would murder Mr. Cantrell, I'd have to say yes. I think he is quite capable of it. Maybe the others would too. I don't know. But if you could have seen him on the beach this afternoon—" She shuddered and was silent.

Dr. Murdock nodded and once more strode the length of the room and back before he asked, "Do you think he has a chance to get at the patient?"

"Not while Stepp is on guard," Susan answered swiftly. "And Stepp will be as long as those three are in the house."

"Good!" The scowl on Dr. Murdock's

fade lifted slightly. "Who prepares the patient's food?"

"Elizabeth and I," Susan answered.

"The tray is prepared in the kitchen and taken straight to the patient?" Dr. Murdock was now every inch the attending physician, interrogating the nurse on duty. "It's never put down somewhere unattended for so much as a moment?"

Susan shook her head. "I take it to him myself," she answered. "It's never out of my sight from the moment Elizabeth and I get it ready until it is served to him."

Dr. Murdock nodded, satisfied.

"Then I can't see that we have too much to worry about," he told her.

"And you don't think I was a fool to get upset? Grady really scared me. I suppose I should be ashamed to admit that, but there was something so evil about him," Susan said, and added impulsively, "I've never thought of myself as an unduly imaginative nurse, but somehow it seems to me there's been an evil atmosphere in the house since they arrived."

Dr. Murdock shook his head. "You're not unduly imaginative, Susan. I felt it, too, and I can't afford to be imaginative. It's there like a sort of fog. I've seen it before when a group of relatives are sitting around waiting for a rich man to die, so they can get their claws on all that he is leaving behind."

He smiled at her wryly and added, "That's something you and I won't ever have to worry about, Susan. We'll never have enough money to tempt greedy relatives."

"It doesn't take an awful lot to stir up greedy relatives," she reminded him ruefully. "I've seen some most unpleasant family battles over a few bits and pieces of linens, a ring worth twenty dollars."

"So have I," he admitted, and drew her up beside him. Once again his arms went about her, holding her gently against him, while with a handful of tissues he mopped her face and bent his head, totally un-expectedly, to set his mouth on hers in a kiss that startled as much as it thrilled her.

"Why, Doctor Murdock!" she managed as she drew herself free of him and stared up at him, wide-eyed, feeling her face hot with color.

He grinned at her, as abashed as a small boy caught stealing cookies, and said quietly, "I'm not going to apologize. I liked it too much. And it's something I've been wanting to do for a long time! Forgive me if you like; I won't say I'm sorry!"

Susan put up shaking hands, laid them against her hot face, and made her eyes meet his, a hint of a vagrant dimple in her cheek as she smiled faintly.

"Who's asking you to?" she drawled, and neatly sidestepped as he reached for her again. "Please, Scott. Someone might come in. Think how it would look if you were caught kissing your nurse!"

"The scandal would rock the island," he told her solemnly, his eyes twinkling. "I shudder to think what the results

134

might be. You might even have to marry me, to salvage my reputation."

Susan laughed unsteadily. "And what about mine?"

"Well, marrying me might save yours, too," he agreed. And then he looked startled as he straightened and the laughter ended. "But why are we standing here lally-gagging?"

"Oh," asked Susan gently, eyebrows raised, "is that what we are doing?"

Once more she had to evade his outstretched hands, and then she, too, became serious.

"You're right, Doctor."

"Surely a nurse who's just been kissed could make it 'Scott'?" he interposed gently.

Color was high in her face, but her eyes were quite steady and increasingly grave as she looked up at him.

"We're standing here making jokes," she began.

"Oh, is that what we are doing?" he asked softly.

"Our patient may need us," she went

on, ignoring his question. "Please, Scott, if you're free, let's get started. I'm afraid to be away from the Cedars too long."

Instantly all hint of teasing, of laughter vanished. Dr. Murdock disappeared into his private office and came back, wearing his suit jacket instead of his white coat and carrying his black bag.

Outside, as he put her into his car, his hands were very gentle, and the look in his eyes lingered on her soft mouth like a caress.

"We must take up where we left off, Susan, and very soon," he told her as he started the car and headed toward the Cedars. "We can't leave a situation like that hanging unresolved in the air, you know."

"But it was only a joke," Susan began uneasily.

"Now you *are* talking like a fool, Susie, my girl." There was more than a hint of resentment in his voice. "You know darned well what happened to me the first time I set eyes on you."

"How could I? You've never even hinted," she stammered.

"Well, where's that celebrated woman's intuition I've heard so much about?" he demanded. "What did I have to do to make you aware of the way I felt? Drop on one knee, with a hand on my heart, and tell you I'd been looking for you all my life and now that I've found you I don't intend ever to let you go again?"

"Well, it would have been helpful if you had," she pointed out.

He took his eyes from the road to give her a glance that was halfway between exasperation and amusement.

"Never you mind!" he warned her. "One of these days I'll get you to myself again, and there will no longer be any doubt about the way I feel toward you. I already know that you aren't engaged or even keeping what the kids call 'steady company.'"

"How do you know that?"

"I asked Mr. Cantrell, of course; how else?"

She caught her breath, and her eyes widened.

"So that's why he asked me so many questions before we came to the Cedars! He said it was so he could be sure I wouldn't have any family calls that would take me away unexpectedly or any boy friends who would be jealous."

Dr. Murdock chuckled. "He asked the questions I was afraid to ask, because of what you might answer."

The car turned between the tall tabby-brick gate posts into the winding drive that led up to the house. Dusk was gathering now, and the house looked serene and peaceful and very beautiful. The lawn was shadowed by the tall cedars, and birds were flitting about them, making their usual night-time racket as they fought over roosting places.

As the car reached the steps, they got out quickly and went into the house. Joyce was in the library, and as she heard the sound of their entrance she came to the hall and eyed them both with a hostility that Susan could almost feel.

138

"I must say, for two who are treating a patient in the condition of Uncle Gerry, his doctor and his nurse are certainly very casual in their care of him," she drawled. Her eyes went from one to the other, and she added, "Really, Doctor, that's not your shade of lipstick at all. It doesn't do a thing for you."

Susan caught her breath as she saw Dr. Murdock's hand go up swiftly to touch his cheek and heard Joyce's insolent laugh. There was, of course, no lipstick on his cheek, but his instinctive gesture had told Joyce what she wanted to know.

"I don't suppose it would do any good if I were to ask you how soon the boys and I may plan to leave?" she went on after a moment.

"Any time you like, Mrs. Gilbert. Make any plans you wish," said Dr. Murdock stiffly.

"You mean Uncle's worse?" she cried swiftly.

"I mean he's doing just fine, and there's really no use your staying around any longer. Feel free to leave any time you like," said Dr. Murdock coolly, and strode to the door of the sick room, which Stepp opened for him immediately.

"Here, you, Nurse! Wait a minute. I want to talk to you." Joyce laid a detaining hand on Susan's arm as she would have followed Dr. Murdock.

Susan freed her arm from Joyce's ungentle grasp and lifted her head.

"I'm afraid I can't think of anything we have to discuss, Mrs. Gilbert," said Susan coldly. "I have to look after my patient."

"Is that why you went high-tailing it off to the village more than an hour ago —so you could look after your patient? You have a weird way of attending to your duties, Nurse!" snapped Joyce.

Stung, Susan said swiftly, "As a matter of fact, Mrs. Gilbert, my trip to the village was in the interest of my patient."

"And not so you could have a nice little private visit with the nice young doctor? Oh, come now, Nurse!" mocked Joyce.

Beyond Joyce, Susan saw a shadow. Grady was standing there, and his eyes on Susan were livid with hate. It was a look

140

that was searing and that caused Susan's nerves to tense. For a moment she looked straight into those hate-filled eyes and realized that Grady knew she had gone straight to Dr. Murdock with an account of the scene on the beach and his own damning words. It was a knowledge that hung between them as though it had been printed on the very air. Then Grady's lips curled in a smile of profound contempt and he turned away as though he had lost interest.

Joyce, too, studied Susan for another moment, then lifted her shoulders in a shrug and turned back to her brothers.

As Susan escaped thankfully to the sick room, she heard Joyce say, in a tone that was obviously meant for her to hear, "I don't trust that nurse one single tiny bit."

And Grady's answer was as obviously meant for her; a drawling, contemptuous, "Who does, except maybe our dedicated young doctor?"

"Probably because they are working together—" Joyce's voice was cut off as

Stepp closed the door of the sick room behind Susan.

For a moment Susan stood very still, her hands over her face, feeling as though she had walked through slime and some of it had clung to her. Stepp looked at her with sympathy and understanding, and Susan made herself smile at him as she lifted her shoulders and tried to shake off the unpleasant effects of her brush with Gerard's "family."

8

AFTER Dr. Murdock had checked Gerard's condition and Susan ascertained by the expression on his face that the condition was satisfactory, she walked with him to the door where Stepp was on guard.

"Continue the medication and treatment, Nurse," said Dr. Murdock, his tone calmly professional, brisk, but his eyes on Susan so touched with ardor that the color rose in her face and her eyes fell shyly away from his. "I'll be back in the morning. Earlier, if you need me."

"Yes, Doctor," said Susan demurely, and for a moment let her eyes meet his. And then he was gone, and she turned back to the bed.

"Like him, don't you, Susie?" asked Gerard's tired voice, touched with a bit of humor that was one of his most endearing characteristics."

"Dr. Murdock?" she asked innocently. "Oh, yes, I've told you before. He seems quite competent and knowledgeable."

"And a darned attractive young man," said Gerard and grinned as the color rose in her face. "You are a very remarkable young woman, Susan. Did you know that?"

"I'm not at all, Mr. Cantrell! But thanks for thinking so!"

"You don't even want to know why I think you are remarkable?"

"Well, of course I'm interested, even though I know it isn't true."

"You're remarkable because you haven't lost the ability to blush" said Gerard. "It's a delightful trait that I thought was entirely lost in these times. I can remember when I was a young man, girls blushed at things they nowadays accept as routine. But you! Scott Murdock is a very lucky young man, Susan."

Susan waited, her hands clenched in the pockets of her uniform. She didn't dare ask what he meant, for she suspected that she already knew. After a moment Gerard chuckled.

"You're not even going to ask me why I think he is lucky?" he teased her.

"I imagine because he's able to do a job he loves, thanks to your backing and support."

"Come off it, Susie, m'girl! You know darned well I meant nothing of the kind," Gerard scoffed. "Scott Murdock is a lucky man because you are in love with him."

The color rushed into Susan's face.

"And he's crazy about you," he went on. "If I had planned the whole thing, it couldn't possibly have worked out more to my liking. The two of you together will be a team that can create miracles of healing! I have great faith in you, Susan —both of you."

"That's very sweet of you, Mr. Cantrell, and I'm very grateful for both of us. I know Scott will be as touched and pleased to hear that as I am," Susan told him with deep appreciation. "I'll get your supper tray now."

She smiled at him, tucked the covers neatly across his chest and went out.

In the kitchen, Elizabeth looked up from the final preparations for dinner for the guests and said grimly, "I suppose you haven't got a nice little bit of poison I could sprinkle in this?"

"I'm afraid not, and the authorities wouldn't approve," Susan answered lightly.

"Well, that's only because the authorities don't know this gang the way I do," said Elizabeth, and added, as Susan began preparing Gerard's tray, "Get your shopping all done?"

Startled, Susan asked, "Shopping?"

"Wasn't that why you had to go to the village?" asked Elizabeth.

"Oh, well, yes—" Susan broke off, and added honestly, "I went to the village because I wanted a private conference with Dr. Murdock."

Elizabeth nodded, obviously not surprised.

"That's what I thought, when Sandy came back and said he had let you out at

146

Doc's office and you'd catch a ride with him when he came out," she said quietly, and stood erect, her fists balled on her hips, her eyes meeting Susan's. "Miss Merrill, Sandy and me feel like there's something going on here that we don't understand but that it's a danger to the chief. We want to help, if there is any such thing going on and we want to be told what we have to do. I still think a sprinkling of poison might not be a bad idea"

Susan put her arm about the woman and hugged her lightly.

"Take my word for it, Elizabeth, there's a much better way to protect Mr. Cantrell. And I'm sure Doctor Murdock will find it," she said quietly.

Elizabeth sighed. "Well, if he can't, nobody can. I'd better start feeding the guests."

"And I'd better start feeding my patient." Susan smiled at her as she picked up the tray.

Elizabeth cast a disparaging eye over

the contents of the tray and shook her head.

"When I think of the meals I used to prepare for the chief and how he used to enjoy them, it fair makes me sick to see the kind of pap Doc feels he should have now," she said and added more brightly, "Maybe a little later on he can have some of the things he likes?"

"We hope so, Elizabeth; we really hope so!" Susan assured her.

Back in the sick room, she smiled at Stepp and said "You'd better go for a walk before dinner, Stepp. You haven't been out of this room all day."

"She's right, Stepp. You go ahead. Susan can take care of me until you get back," Gerard added his endorsement.

Stepp hesitated and looked sharply at Susan.

"Think you can hold the fort, miss?" he asked.

"I'll lock the door the minute you leave, and I won't unlock it until you get back," Susan promised him.

Startled, Gerard looked from her to

Stepp, but neither of them was aware of the glance. When Stepp had gone and the door had been locked behind him, Susan came back beside the bed where Gerard was propped up, the bed tray across his knees.

He looked up at her, showing no interest at all in the food, and asked quietly, "Is it as bad as that?"

Puzzled, Susan asked, "As bad as what?"

"So bad that I have to be locked in my room away from my loving family." Gerard's faint hesitation before the last word was brilliantly illuminating.

"It's just that we don't want them to disturb you," she began.

But Gerard had lost interest. He picked at the food. When she took the tray away he looked up at her suddenly, a faint scowl drawing his brows together, his jaw set hard beneath his pallid face.

"I've been thinking, Susan," he told her.

"Well, so long as you don't work too hard at it." She smiled.

"I've been thinking that I'd like to have my lawyer come down and bring my will so I can make some changes," he said. "What would you say if I told you I'm thinking very seriously of making *you* my heir?"

Susan stared at him, shocked and dismayed.

"Don't you dare!" she burst out sharply.

His brows went up slightly.

"Don't you want to be rich, Susan?"

"Of course I don't!" she gasped. "I wouldn't know what to do with a lot of money. Why, Mr. Cantrell, if you left me so much as five dollars those people in there would tear me to bits! They are your heirs and they are counting definitely on inheriting." She broke off because she hadn't meant to reveal so much of her secret feelings against the others.

"I've taken good care of them, Susan," Gerard told her. "I've done more for them than they had any right to expect. David is a fine lawyer, working with one of the most respected firms in New York.

Joyce has had everything any sane woman could want; there is a trust fund set up for the little girl that is irrevocable and from which she will get the income as long as she lives. And there is also adequate provision for Grady, who doesn't seem able to make up his mind what he wants to do with his life. So why shouldn't I do what I want with what's left?"

"There's no reason at all, of course. But *please*, Mr. Cantrell, don't leave any of it to me!" Susan pleaded earnestly. "There are very unpleasant consequences when a nurse inherits a large sum of money from a patient; don't do that to me, please!"

Gerard studied her, frowning.

"You really mean that, don't you, Susan?" he asked after a moment.

"Believe me, Mr. Cantrell, I never meant anything more," she assured him so earnestly that he could not doubt her.

"Then of course I won't." He smiled faintly. "It's just that I've always loved the Cedars so much, and I hoped that

151

someone would come after me who would love it and want to live here when I've finished with it. But if you don't want it, then that's that."

"Mr. Cantrell, the Cedars is the loveliest place I've ever known and I *do* love it very much," Susan told him quite honestly. "I can't think of anything I'd like better than for it to be my home as long as I live. But I'm a nurse, Mr. Cantrell. I've been one so long, it's all I know. So even if the Cedars belonged to me, I couldn't live here and still be a nurse. You do understand, don't you?"

Gerard's smile was faint, and he turned his head away as though he were very tired.

"Of course, my dear, of course," he told her. "It was just a thought, an idle one born of an old man's weariness and illness. And why are we worrying about changing my will now? You and Scott assure me I've got several more years of life, and that's ample time for any changes I might want to make. I think I'll get some sleep now."

Susan made him comfortable, set the tray aside to be taken to the kitchen when Stepp returned, and sat down in the corner, beyond the reach of the small bedside lamp that pushed the shadows away from the bed.

She sighed happily and settled herself cozily, until she heard Stepp's cautious touch at the door and rose to let him in.

Stepp closed the door behind him without a sound, and his eyes went swiftly to the bed.

"How is he?" he asked as though he had been gone days rather than less than an hour.

"Fine," Susan murmured. "He's sleeping soundly, and the fever is way down. I'll take the supper tray back to the kitchen. Be sure to call me, Stepp, if you need me."

"Sure, miss, sure," Stepp told her, and settled himself for the night's vigil he would not surrender to anyone.

As Susan went across the big reception hall and down to the kitchen, she heard voices in the living room. She hurried, trying to block her ears so that she could not distinguish words in what was obviously an acrimonious debate. But then, she asked herself dryly as she pushed open the swinging door into the kitchen, had she ever heard them in anything but an angry debate?

Elizabeth sat with her shoes off, beneath the light in the breakfast room, the daily newspaper that came by boat each day from the mainland unfolded in her hands. She popped her spectacles up over her forehead and stood up as Susan came in bearing the tray.

"Guess he wasn't hungry!" she commented. "Shame, too, when he needs to eat to get his strength back. Here, you go sit down; I'll wash up."

"You sit down and I'll wash up," Susan ordered as she scraped the dishes and deposited them in the sink, beneath a stream of hot water. "I imagine you've been washing up for the last hour, haven't you?"

"Well, just about," Elizabeth answered, and added, lowering her voice,

154

"Sandy was serving dinner to 'em, and he says they're sure in a stew. That David says he's got to get back to handle a mighty important case; and that Mrs. Gilbert says she's been invited by friends on a world cruise aboard their yacht, and if she is not in New York ready to sail by the last of next week, they'll go off and leave her. And that Grady just sits there with a face a foot long and scowls at everybody and says nothing. But I bet he's got some mighty fancy plans of his own, don't you?"

And remembering the scene with Grady on the beach, Susan said quietly, "I'm sure he has."

Elizabeth watched Susan as she washed the delicate china and the heirloom silver that had been on Gerard's tray. Suddenly she said softly, but with a deep-rooted resentment, "They just make me sick— sitting around waiting for the chief to go. As good as he has been to them all these years, you'd think they'd have a little kindness toward him, now wouldn't you?"

Susan set her teeth, counted to ten and reminded herself that she must control her tongue.

"What's happened to the little girl? I haven't seen her around," she managed to ask.

"Oh, Maisie's practicing on her," said Elizabeth carelessly.

"Practicing on her?" Susan repeated, puzzled.

Elizabeth grinned.

"Maisie's studying to be a teacher, and she said she'd likely have a lot of spoiled and pampered first graders, maybe even kindergarteners, to contend with, and she might as well find out right now if she was going to be able to handle 'em. She said it seemed like that small imp was as good an example as she was likely to find anywhere. So from the very first she's been looking after the kid. I must say she's tamed her right smart, too, a heap sight more than I ever expected anybody could do. Says all the child needs is a lot of love, which it's plain she's not getting from that mother of hers."

"I think Maisie will make an excellent teacher," Susan said.

"Well, it's what she wants to do, and as soon as she takes her board examinations this fall, she'll be given a school somewhere. Just hope she's going to like it as much as she thinks she will."

"Oh, I think she will," Susan answered, and put the last of the silver in readiness for Gerard's breakfast tray in the morning. "I'll check with Stepp and then I'll go to bed, so I can relieve him early. I've tried to get him to let me take the night shift, but he refuses. Says he's always been where Mr. Cantrell can reach him without so much as calling out, and now more than any other time he's going to keep on doing that."

Elizabeth nodded agreement. "He's a fine man, Stepp is," she said and grinned as Susan flung her a startled glance. "Oh, we have our piddling little arguments, mostly where the chief can hear, because seems like he gets a big bang out of listening to us. But Stepp and me, we're mighty good friends, underneath!"

"No one would ever guess it from the way you bicker." Susan laughed as she said good night, and Elizabeth went back to reading her paper.

"I might as well just sit here till the company settles down for the night," Elizabeth told her. "I'd no more than get straight in bed before they'd start ringing bells and demanding a snack! I put my foot down on them raiding the icebox, because they never remember to shut the door, and when I get in the kitchen in the morning the freezer is thawed down and the place looks like a flock of locusts had been visiting."

"You really should get your rest, Elizabeth. You've been up and going since daylight, I happen to know," Susan protested.

"There'll be plenty of time for me to rest one of these days," said Elizabeth somberly, and Susan felt the prick of tears behind her eyelids as she went out and down the hall to the sick room.

Stepp opened the door for her and said softly, "He's sleeping like a baby, miss.

You go along and get your sleep. I'll call you if we need you."

"You promise, Stepp?"

He looked surprised. "Well, sure I promise, miss!"

Susan checked and was deeply relieved to discover that the pulse and respiration of the patient were good. Then she nodded good night to Stepp and went to her own room.

159

9

FOR a few uneasy days, the situation did not change. Dr. Murdock was pleased with the way the patient was responding to the treatment, and Gerard smiled warmly when an examination was finished and said firmly, "I'm going to make it, boy! First thing you know, I'll be off on that world cruise I've always wanted to make."

"Another one?" Scott mocked him as he stowed his equipment in his bag. "Seems to me you have made two or three since I've known you."

Gerard chuckled. "But the world keeps changing, boy! Each time I go I find things I hadn't known about; or find things I had known and loved were no longer there! No, I think I'll make one more cruise and then settle down."

Outside the room, as Susan was following Scott to receive any instructions for the patient's care that he might wish to give her, Joyce Gilbert was waiting for them. And just behind her in the library, Susan saw the two men.

"See here, Doctor, we can't hang around here the rest of our lives," Joyce snapped.

Behind her David asked, his voice trying unsuccessfully to drown hers, "How is he this morning, Doctor?"

Dr. Murdock looked from one to the other, and Susan felt she had never admired him more than when he said cheerfully, "Why, he's fine! He's doing even better than I had expected; almost as well as I had hoped."

Susan, standing a pace behind him, saw the flicker of expression—disappointment? anger? resentment?—that sped across the three faces as they exchanged swift glances.

It was once more David who spoke, as though he had elected himself spokesman for his brother and sister. "Then there *is* some hope that he may pull through, in spite of what Dr. Willard at the hospital in Atlanta told us?"

Dr. Murdock said quietly, "There is excellent hope that he may have a few more good years. He is talking of taking a world cruise."

"A *what?*" Joyce blazed. "He must be out of his mind. A man in a dying condition wanting to make a world cruise! It mustn't be permitted."

Dr. Murdock smiled at her, though his eyes were bleak and cold.

"But you see, Mrs. Gilbert, he is no longer in a dying condition," he told her. "I agree with you that a long journey wouldn't be advisable, of course."

"Or possible, would it?" demanded David baldly.

"Well, it's difficult to say, Mr. Barford, what is possible and what is impossible." Dr. Murdock's tone was polite, even suave. "I don't think he has any intention of going anywhere. He loves the Cedars so much that I think he'd be perfectly happy just to potter about here and bask in his memories."

Joyce sneered, "Bask in his memories? What a pretty thought, Doctor."

"Thank you, Mrs. Gilbert." Dr. Murdock's smile was pleasant, but his eyes were not.

'I'm afraid we'll have to be leaving tomorrow, Doctor." David once more tried to pour oil on the troubled waters roiled by Joyce's unpleasant manner. "I have an important case coming up the first of the week, and I have to do some research on it before I go into court. And my sister has social obligations, as does my brother. You feel it would be safe for us to leave tomorrow, don't you?"

Susan's heart leaped, but she kept her hands tightly clenched in her pockets as she waited for Dr. Murdock to answer David. Scott hesitated for just the right length of time and then said pleasantly, "Why, I am sure it will, Mr. Barford. Everything possible is being done for Mr. Cantrell and will continue to be done. And of course, should there be a need, we can get in touch with you, I'm sure."

"Yes, of course," said David and turned back to the library.

"If you think for one single moment you can get us down here on another wild-goose chase—" Joyce began belligerently even as David's hand closed hard on her arm.

"Now, Joyce, it wasn't Dr. Murdock who sent for us, remember? Dr. Willard felt that, as Uncle Gerry's only relatives, we would want to be here—and of course he was perfectly right. But now that we know there is nothing we can do for him, nothing that we're allowed to do, the best thing for us is to get packed and make arrangements to leave in the morning," he told her harshly, and dismissed Dr. Murdock with a curt, "Good day, Doctor."

Susan and Dr. Murdock walked out of the house and stood for a moment beside his car. Susan put her hands over her face as Dr. Murdock stood looking down at her with that warm, ardent look that gave wings to her heart.

"It's been rough, honey, but by this

164

time tomorrow they will be gone," he told her softy.

"I suppose it's silly of me to be so upset about the way they are acting, but I have grown very fond of Mr. Cantrell. He's such a grand person! And to have them sitting around, waiting for him to die, angry because he doesn't—*ugh!*"

Dr. Murdock said dryly, "Remind me some day to tell you about the old girl who came with her husband of forty years to discuss an operation for the removal of cataracts that were dooming him to blindness; and when she was told what the operation would cost, she asked innocently, 'But, Doctor, wouldn't it be a lot cheaper to hire somebody to lead him around?'"

Susan stared at him, wide-eyed.

"Oh, Scott, *no!*" she gasped.

"Fact, I assure you, and not a very pretty one," he told her, and his jaw was set and hard as though just remembering the case made him feel slightly sick.

Susan drew a deep, hard breath.

"Well, if having money makes people

165

that hard and callous, I'm glad we'll never have any!" she said half under her breath.

Dr. Murdock grinned at her in an effort to lift her spirits.

"Oh, I wouldn't say that," he told her teasingly. "After all, I've known doctors who drove imported sports cars and draped their wives in mink and went away for weekends on fancy yachts."

"Not our kind of doctors," she insisted firmly. "We're not going to be 'society doctors' treating imaginary ailments of overstuffed women who need nothing but some good, hard exercise, but insist on being given fancy drugs so they can reduce without dieting."

She broke off because he was laughing at her and stared at him resentfully.

"What's so funny?" she demanded.

"You are! 'Our kind of doctor' indeed!" he teased her. "Does that mean that you're going to marry me, as I've been hoping?"

Scarlet with confusion, she stammered, "Well, golly, yes. Isn't that what we've been planning?"

"I have," he assured her. "But I wasn't sure you were until now. I've been hoping, but haven't quite dared to plan. But now I can! And believe me, I will!"

Susan was dewy-eyed, still flushed, and her answer came in a whisper. "I'm glad. I should have waited for you to propose to me, all formal and everything, I suppose. I guess I—well, sort of jumped the gun, didn't I?"

Dr. Murdock's grin was teasing. "I'm afraid you did, sweet thing," he told her, and his voice was so low that it was barely able to carry the weight of the tenderness he gave it. "I'll remind you of that some day; the very first time we quarrel!"

"Oh, but we won't quarrel!" she protested. "Not ever!"

"Be a bit dull and stodgy if we don't, won't it?"

"Oh, no. Being married to you couldn't ever be dull or stodgy. It'll be too much fun!" she assured him earnestly.

"That," said Dr. Murdock, and for a moment his hand closed on hers and held it tightly, "is the nicest thing anyone ever said to me. I'd like so much to kiss you, darling. But there are probably spies lurking in the shrubbery."

"Probably," she agreed reluctantly, and gave him a smile that was as ardent as a caress. "But they'll be gone tomorrow."

"And we'll be here," she told him softly, and smiled contentedly at him.

He gave her hand a tight pressure, smiled down at her and got into his car. She stood where she was, hands in her pockets, watching as the car slid down the drive in the late afternoon sunlight. She was in no hurry to return to the house with its pervading atmosphere of evil. She tried to tell herself that she was being melodramatic, but she shivered at the many evidences the relatives of that kind, gentle sweet old man had offered of their completely callous attitude toward him.

She turned at last and went back to the house and was grateful that she reached the sick room without having to see any of the three.

Stepp stood up as she came in and moved swiftly to lock the door.

"They're leaving tomorrow, Stepp," Susan murmured, and saw the joy and relief that flooded Stepp's ugly face.

From the bed, Gerard's voice reached them. Startled, Susan moved swiftly to him.

"Is that true, Susie?" he asked, his voice so husky that she had to lean low to hear.

"Is what true, Mr. Cantrell?" she asked gently.

"That my loving relatives are checking out?"

"Well, yes, Mr. Cantrell. It seems they have business that is urgent and they must go." Susan's lame explanation broke down beneath the sardonic gleam in his eye.

"Haven't time or patience to wait for the old man to up and die, eh? Well, you might tell them I have every intention of living until I can make some changes in my will," he told her firmly.

Alarmed, Susan protested, "Now, Mr. Cantrell, you promised."

His chuckle was so soft that but for the

impish twinkle in his eyes she could not have been quite sure she heard it.

"Oh, yes, I promised, Susie, my girl and I'll keep my promise," he assured her. "Matter of fact, I've been lying here thinking over the will, and I have about decided it's the way I want it. You remember the day my attorney came to the hospital, very soon after I'd been admitted? I was pretty sure then what I wanted. And I'm more certain now than I was then."

"That's good," smiled Susan. "Would you like something to eat? Perhaps an eggnog? Or some orange juice?"

"Too close to supper time, Susie. I don't want to spoil my appetite for that deliciously appetizing goo you poke at me three times a day!" he mocked.

"I'll make you a promise. The very first time Dr. Murdock says you may have solid food, I'll see to it that you get the largest and noblest steak the market affords, broiled as only Elizabeth can do it," Susan assured him.

"That's a promise to dream about,

Susie. And don't think I won't hold you to it, before many more days," he told her. "How about reading me the morning paper? Has it come?"

"Oh, yes, I'll get it," Susan told him, and hurried across to the library and the rack where the daily paper was always stored.

Even as she searched for it, Grady Barford's voice spoke from the terrace as he held up the paper.

"This what you're looking for?"

"Why, yes, it is. Mr. Cantrell would like me to read it to him." Susan came out to the terrace through the open French doors and held out her hand for the paper. "I hope you've finished with it?"

He thrust it into her hand, and then his hand closed on hers and held her prisoner for a moment. His face was dark and ugly with anger as he glared down at her.

"Of course I know you 'ratted' on me to that medico of yours, and probably to Uncle Gerry as well," he sneered at her. "What's all this nonsense about a nurse keeping her mouth shut about the affairs of the patient's family?"

"I did not 'rat' on you, as you express it."

"You're lying! You rushed straight to the village and spilled the whole thing to that quack doctor."

"He's not a quack! He's a very fine doctor, and you should be grateful to him for all that he's doing for your uncle."

"Oh, sure, sure! I'm all broken out with gratitude for losing the money I begged, borrowed and scraped together to put into that option," Grady said between his teeth. "And now that you and your precious doctor have patched Uncle up so he's going to outlive all of us, I suppose you are very proud of yourselves!"

Susan wrenched her arm free of his grasp and, with blazing eyes, said hotly, "We certainly are! And if you had any normal feeling for him at all, you'd be grateful to us!"

Grady swore under his breath. "Grateful, she says!"

Susan eyed him for a moment with sick

disgust before she turned and went back to the sick room.

Gerard eyed her as she seated herself beside the bed and unfolded the newspaper.

"Something upset you, Susie?" he asked quietly.

"Oh, no, it was just that the paper wasn't where I expected it to be and I had to hunt for it," she assured him with an airiness that did not convince him in the least, though he did not pursue the subject further. "Let's see, what would you like first? The stock market? The front page?"

Gerard said gently, "The society page, please."

Susan stared at him, her brows raised.

Gerard grinned. "I always like to know who's getting married and who's entertaining for the bride-elect and who's been seen where with whom," he told her pleasantly.

"You don't mean that!" Susan scoffed.

"Fact, I assure you," he told her, and all raillery vanished from his voice as he

173

went on. "It takes my mind off the sorry state of affairs in the world: the race question; the arms race; the Cuban situation; the labor situation; murders and violence. I find it very comforting that while the world is, to use an old-fashioned phrase, going to hell in a basket, there are starry-eyed brides and grooms and charitable committees of the various women's organizations having fashion shows and teas and giving parties and introducing daughters to society. It's so obvious that no matter what calamitous events are taking place over the world, women everywhere are determined to ignore them and to go on living as if there would be no terrible tomorrow."

"But, Mr. Cantrell, we can't all crawl into caves and weep and bewail the end of the world as we have known it," Susan said earnestly. "The world has been here for a long, long time. I have complete confidence that it will be here for a long time to come. Oh, sure, I know there is grave danger all over the world. But

174

we've come out of these things before; we'll come out of these."

Gerard studied her curiously. "You're young, Susie; frighteningly young, I sometimes think."

"Well," Susan assured him sunnily, though there was anxiety in her eyes, "that's something time will take care of, isn't it?"

"That it will, Susie m'girl, that it will." He sighed and grimaced. "Well, shall we see what's going on in the realm of what's politely known as society?"

"Of course, if that's what you want," Susan agreed.

She felt a trifle silly reading the somewhat fulsome account of a wedding; entertainments for prospective brides; the various committees who were planning charity benefits. But she soon sensed that he wasn't really listening anyway. His eyes held a far-away look, as though he were absorbed in thoughts that were not too pleasant. And so she lowered her voice to an almost hypnotic tone and soon realized, with relief, that he was asleep.

She sat studying him. In the far corner of the room, the ever-present Stepp hovered.

10

AT a little before ten Susan assured herself that everything she could do for Gerard to give him a comfortable night had been done, and she said good night to Stepp, exacting the usual promise from him that if the slightest need for her services arose he would summon her at once.

She lay awake for a little while and had just drifted off to sleep when there was a low, insistent knock on her door and Stepp's urgent voice, "Miss Merrill, come quick. The chief—"

Instantly alert as her training had taught her, she at once got out of bed and into her tailored robe, thrust her feet into slippers and ran along the corridor behind Stepp.

He held open the door for her, and her first glance told her that Gerard was in extremity.

"Call Dr. Murdock, Stepp." She spoke over her shoulder as she ran toward the bed.

"I already did, miss, before I called you. Knew it'd take him a little while to get here," Stepp said hurriedly.

Susan's heart sank as she reached the bed. The thing that she knew Dr. Murdock had dreaded above everything else was the occurrence of emboli: small fragments of the growths on the valves of the heart that break off and may appear in various parts of the body. Just where this one had been carried by the blood stream she could not be sure. But she was so certain that this was what had happened that when Dr. Murdock arrived a few minutes later she looked up at him, white-faced, above her dark robe.

"It's an embolus, isn't it?" she whispered.

Dark-faced, his eyes bitter, Dr. Murdock said, "Yes. In the brain, I feel sure. There's paralysis. I was afraid of this yesterday when I discovered the petechiae. They were on the chest, below the collar bone."

"I know," said Susan huskily. "Tiny red dots not bigger than a pinhead. But he'd had them before and they'd gone away."

There was little they could do for Gerard; both had known from the moment they entered the room that his disease had reached its terminal point.

When it was all over, Susan turned wordlessly to Dr. Murdock, and his arms enfolded her. His face was twisted with a bitterness which hurt Susan almost as much as Gerard's death.

"Oh, Scott darling, don't feel so badly! You did everything you could, and we're not God! All we can do is use all the skill and ability we may have and leave the rest to Him!" she pleaded.

"I know, but I promised him a few more years. And he *trusted* me." Deep hurt was in Dr. Murdock's husky voice. And then Stepp, at the foot of the bed, tears running unashamedly down his weathered face, spoke.

"You got no call to feel bad, Doc," he told Scott. "The chief's been hurting bad for a long time and didn't say much about it. But he's free now. He's not hurting any more. I guess maybe this is the way he would want it to be. He thought a lot of you, Doc."

"And I thought a lot of him, Stepp," said Dr. Murdock huskily. "I never hated to lose a patient in all my life as much as I hated to lose him, Stepp. If he had been my own father—" His voice broke and he set his jaw hard and breathed deeply.

Stepp said quietly after a moment, "I'd better let Elizabeth and Sandy know."

He opened the door and went out, and this time, though he closed it, he did not lock it.

He had been gone only a few minutes when the door was thrust violently open and David, Grady and Joyce stood there, in hastily donned robes, Joyce with her face cold-creamed, a chin strap fastened beneath it.

"We heard the commotion," David began. The next moment his eyes found the still, calm face of his uncle, and saw he was still and rigid. "So he's gone," he said very softly.

Susan looked from one to the other and saw a relief that was almost delight in their avid faces She turned away, sickened at the sight.

"So your little guinea pig scheme didn't work after all, eh, Doc?" David's voice was almost a purr. The others fastened their eyes on Dr. Murdock, and Susan felt she could all but hear them lick their chops. "We'll demand an autopsy, of course."

Startled, scowling, Dr. Murdock repeated incredulously, "An autopsy?"

"Well, of course; what else? Here you've been going around assuring us that he would live for several years, and now he's dead, just like that!" David answered, and malice was thick in his voice. "You don't think we are going to let you get away with this, do you! We want to know *why* he died so suddenly, after all the favorable reports you've been giving us about him."

Joyce said uneasily, "Now, David—"

"Shut up," David ordered her sharply. "I'm a lawyer. I know it's against all medical ethics, even against the law, to experiment with a patient without the family's consent. Which you definitely did not have!"

Dr. Murdock met his eyes.

"You're forgetting I had the patient's consent, Mr. Barford," he pointed out. "And when the patient is in full possession of all his faculties, that's all that is required."

"Ah, but that's just the point we must settle. *Was* he in full possession of all his faculties?" demanded David, and grinned malevolently.

Dr. Murdock, startled, scowled at him.

"Are you asking if your uncle was mentally deranged in any way? That's utter nonsense!" he snapped.

"That's something to be settled later. Right now, my brother and my sister and I insist that an autopsy be performed by some thoroughly qualified medical man in whose opinion we can have confidence,"

David insisted. "I'm sure you're sufficiently acquainted with the law as it concerns such things to realize that we have a perfect right to demand such an autopsy."

"You do, of course," said Dr. Murdock grimly. "Matter of fact, I had meant to apply to you for permission to order one. I'd like very much to be sure that it really *was* an embolus—"

"A what?" snapped David sharply.

"In subacute bacterial endocarditis, there is a productive inflammation of the valves of the heart, which causes growths —vegetation if you prefer to call it that —with ulceration of the tissues," Dr. Murdock explained brusquely. "There is an occurrence of emboli, small fragments of the growths about the valves that may break off and be carried to various parts of the body in the bloodstream. They are carried through the arteries and may lodge in some distant part of the body. I believe that in Mr. Cantrell's case, an embolus invaded the brain and brought on paralysis. Naturally, an autopsy will prove or disprove that diagnosis, so I would like very much to have one."

"And you'll get it, just as soon as we can find a medic in whose word we can trust!" drawled David in a tone that made it a verbal slap.

"Then, of course, you will not be leaving tomorrow," said Dr. Murdock.

David exchanged glances with his brother and sister and asked contemptuously, "Can you ask? That's as silly a question as I ever heard. We'll be here until after the funeral, of course, and the reading of the will. And after that I'm sure all three of us hope never to set eyes on this place again. It shouldn't be too much trouble to sell it, if we are willing to take a loss; we will be under the circumstances."

He turned and, followed by the other two, crossed the hall to the library and thrust the door shut.

Susan looked at Dr. Murdock with sick, shocked eyes. But before she could speak Stepp returned with Elizabeth and

Sandy and Maisie, all obviously hastily aroused from sleep.

When, at last, the sad tasks following a death had been attended to and the ambulance had carried Gerard away for the last time from his beloved home, Susan stood beside Dr. Murdock where his car was parked and looked up at him in the moon-silvered darkness.

"They're even more horrible than I thought they were," she admitted, her voice shaking. "And I didn't think that was possible, did you?"

"Well, no," Dr. Murdock admitted. Then suddenly, so unexpectedly that Susan gasped with shock, he added sternly, "You're going to leave the Cedars tomorrow morning, Susan, and go straight back to the hospital."

"Why, I'll do no such thing!" she gasped.

"You will, Susan, because I ask it of you," he told her firmly. "These people are going to be nasty. There's going to be a mess, and I don't want you involved in it."

"But I *am* involved. I was his nurse!"

"Susan, there's going to be a really unpleasant mess about all this," Dr. Murdock insisted, and even in the moonlight she could see his jaw was set and hard. "After all, I did try an experimental drug on him, and without his family's approval or consent."

"But you had his, Scott—his enthusiastic and willing consent."

"So you and I say," he pointed out grimly. "But if they don't choose to take our word for it—"

"But he signed the papers giving his consent and they were witnessed by Stepp and Sandy! They can't deny that!"

"Don't you see what they're aiming at, Susan?"

"I'm not sure of anything except that it will be something evil."

"They're going to try to claim that Mr. Cantrell was not in sound mind when he signed the papers," Dr. Murdock pointed out.

"Oh, Scott, *no!*"

"Oh, Susan, *yes!*" Grimly he mimicked

186

her. "And I don't want you here to get involved."

"Now you're just being silly!" Susan flashed hotly. "I can testify, if it should be necessary, that he was of perfectly sound mind. So can Stepp and Elizabeth and Sandy!"

"Susan, Susan, my precious, don't you understand?" Dr. Murdock was determined to try to make her. "If they make an issue of this, as I'm sure they are, then it isn't going to do my medical reputation any good to have a suit like this. And it will do you no good, either, as a nurse. So you mustn't get involved."

Susan drew a deep, hard breath and clenched her hands tightly in the pockets of her robe, tilting her chin at a defiant angle.

"I love you, Scott," she told him huskily. "And what sort of creep would I be to walk out on you at a time like this? I won't do it, and you're wasting your time trying to make me. I *know* that you had Mr. Cantrell's permission; I *know* he was in his right mind; and I'm going to stay right here so that I can swear to that in front of anybody at all that has a right to ask questions. So that's that! Now hush trying to give me orders!"

The violence of her manner brought a faint glimmer to Dr. Murdock's eyes, and he drew her close and held her, kissed her ardently and said, "Well, if that's the way you feel—"

"It's exactly the way I feel, and don't try to talk me out of it," she told him. "You may as well learn now as later that I'm a pretty stubborn somebody!"

"I'm beginning to get that idea," he told her, and kissed her again.

For a moment they stood close in each other's arms, and then he straightened, let her go and moved toward his car.

"I'd better get going, honey," he told her. "I'll see you tomorrow."

"And tomorrow and tomorrow and tomorrow, world without end, darling." Her voice was so soft, so shaken with tenderness, that he turned once more and held her close. And then he was gone, the red tail light of his car twinkling down the drive and vanishing between the cedars.

Susan turned at last and went back into the house.

189

11

THE autopsy, done by a doctor of David's own choosing from the hospital in Atlanta, confirmed all of Dr. Murdock's findings. In fact, the doctor was considerably incensed that he had been called on a case of Dr. Murdock's and one with which he himself had been familiar at the hospital.

"Of course, Murdock, you do realize, I'm sure, that using that EC 211 was a rather risky thing to do," he said as he was preparing to leave the Cedars. "Oh, I know you had the patient's consent. I'm quite sure he was more than willing. But an experimental drug like that that hadn't been thoroughly tested—"

Dr. Murdock said quietly, as Susan listened tensely, "There's one thing I'd like you to tell me, Doctor. The drug did him no harm, did it?"

Dr. Hudson stared at him, drawing his brows together.

"Are you asking me if it deprived him of a week or two of life, Doctor?" he demanded. "Speeded things up a bit, so to speak?"

"Frankly, yes, that's what I meant," Dr. Murdock answered. "I gave him my word it wouldn't."

Dr. Hudson, a short, stocky man in his fifties who headed the pathology department at the hospital, shot him a stern glance.

"Very unwise of you, Dr. Murdock." He scowled. "But you can relax. It didn't. He lived longer than we at the hospital dared to hope when we let him come home. That's why Dr. Willard was distressed that the relatives should demand an autopsy."

He was thrusting things into his briefcase. He straightened, looked about him and said briskly, "Nice little place you have here, Doctor; just the sort of place I'd like to have waiting when I decide to retire."

191

"As if you ever would!" Susan could not keep back the words, and Dr. Hudson shot her a swift, faintly amused glance.

"I suppose not," he agreed, and turned once more to Dr. Murdock. "It's too bad about the embolus, Doctor. But of course I needn't remind you that's one of the greatest dangers about endocarditis."

Dr. Murdock nodded. "I know, of course. It's just that I had hoped for a miracle, I suppose."

"Don't we all?" Dr. Hudson agreed, and sighed. "We hear very good things about you at the hospital, Doctor. I'm going, with your consent of course, to present your charts on this case and your experiment at the next state board meeting of the Medical Society."

"Even though I failed?"

Dr. Hudson looked distinctly annoyed. "Nonsense, Doctor! If we doctors were afraid of failures we'd never accomplish anything in fighting diseases. Think of all the experiments, the weeks and months of lab. work, that go into the achievement of one tiny victory. Of course there are failures, in any profession. But in ours, if we didn't risk failures, make experiments, medicine would still be back in horse-and-buggy days and we'd have no Salk vaccine, no protection from typhoid fever, malaria, the diseases that a few years ago wiped out thousands. Don't be afraid of failure, Doctor; it's the testing, the trying, the looking ahead that counts."

He straightened, snapped his brief case shut and said briskly, "Well, that's that. Now if you'll get me back to the airport I can still make my twelve o'clock appointment."

Susan and Dr. Murdock drove him to the airport, where the chartered plane that had brought him down was waiting to fly him back to the hospital. As the big silver bird lifted itself into the sky, Susan looked up at Dr. Murdock as she slipped her hand in his and felt the pressure with which his fingers closed over hers.

"Feel better, darling, now that you know the experiment did him no harm?" she asked gently.

Dr. Murdock smiled down at her as he turned and walked with her to the car.

"Much better," he told her. "Now if we can just get past the funeral without the relatives making any more fuss, we'll be able to grieve for the man you and I loved. I doubt there'll be any grieving on their part."

"I know," admitted Susan, and shivered. "Did you see their faces when Dr. Hudson gave them the report of the autopsy findings?"

"I did and wondered what they thought an autopsy would reveal," Dr. Murdock answered grimly.

Susan hesitated, and then, as the car headed back across the bridge, she confessed ruefully, "I'm glad there was an autopsy."

Dr. Murdock stared at her, shocked and mildly resentful.

"Now that's a crazy thing for you to say," he protested.

"Not crazy; just melodramatic." Susan was slightly abashed. "Oh, I know I'm an idiot, but they were so upset when they thought he was getting better; and they were so angry at having to cool their heels and wait for him to die, poor darling."

Dr. Murdock looked down at her, scowling.

"Look here, you haven't been thinking that maybe they could have poisoned him?" he demanded.

"Well, I know it sounds crazy, with Stepp constantly on guard. But honestly, Scott dear, you haven't lived in the house with them the way I have for the last ten days. It seems like a year! I'm convinced they are capable of just about anything that would help them get their hands on the Cantrell estate as fast as possible."

Dr. Murdock said soothingly, "Now, honey, you're all upset and that's understandable. But if knowing the results of the autopsy relieves your mind in the smallest degree, then I'm glad, too, that they asked for it."

Susan reminded him tautly, "You told them that if they hadn't, you were going to."

Dr. Murdock nodded, his brows drawn close together.

"Well, let's just say we were both a bit melodramatic," he agreed. "I didn't know them as well as you did, but I'm quite willing to take your verdict on them. But don't worry, darling. They'll be gone as soon as the funeral is over and the will read. And then you and I can make some plans of our own. And that will be pretty wonderful, won't it?"

Susan drew closer to him and sighed happily, "Oh, yes!"

As they drew up to the entrance of the Cedars, Joyce came swiftly to meet them, a slip of paper in one hand, a pencil in the other.

"Will it be safe for us to set the funeral for ten-thirty in the morning?" she asked briskly. "I've just been talking to Uncle Gerry's attorney, Mr. Lawson, and he won't be able to get here until the morning. Since he and Uncle Gerry were old friends, naturally he'd like to attend the funeral."

"Naturally!" Dr. Murdock's tone was polite but dry.

Joyce ignored that.

"He's bringing Uncle's will, of course. I thought immediately after the funeral, we'd return here for the reading of the will. I've told Elizabeth to prepare lunch. Afterwards, the boys and I will fly back to Atlanta with Mr. Lawson and be able to make connections with one of the New York jets that take off from there three times a day."

Dr. Murdock said quietly, "You're very efficient, Mrs. Gilbert."

Joyce eyed him with a hostile expression.

"Someone has to be, Doctor! And the boys are absolutely no good at such arrangements," she told him haughtily. "The time for the funeral is not too early? I mean, everything can be taken care of by then?"

"I think so," Dr. Murdock told her grimly.

"Good! Then I'll expect you to attend to the details," she went on briskly.

"Here's a list that Mr. Lawson said covered Uncle's wishes about the interment and all. And since you know the village and its people, I'm sure you can arrange to have the crypt ready for him at ten-thirty."

She thrust the paper into Dr. Murdock's hand and went back into the house as Dr. Murdock and Susan exchanged glances that were sick with disgust.

"Of course, somebody has to be efficient at such a time," he tried to lighten the gloom Susan was obviously feeling.

"Yes, but she doesn't have to enjoy it so much!" said Susan, and added, "I don't think I ever really hated anybody before. But I hate them!"

"I know, darling, but it's for only a little while longer, less than twenty-four hours. And than you'll never have to see them again."

"And won't that be wonderful?" said Susan.

After he had gone she went unwillingly

198

back into the house, where once again she met Joyce, rushing briskly about.

"Oh," said Joyce, and gave her a nasty smile, "will you be staying on for the funeral?"

"Of course. Did you doubt it?" demanded Susan.

Joyce's eyes swept over her and dismissed her.

"Well, of course you are no longer on salary," she drawled. "But I see no reason why you shouldn't spend the night here and leave tomorrow after the funeral. Though I should think you'd be anxious to get back to the hospital and a new job."

"Do you?" Susan answered coolly. "My job at the hospital is waiting for me, *if* I decide to go back."

Joyce's penciled brows went up.

"Oh, you aren't sure? I suppose you and this young doctor have plans?" Joyce's tone was frankly insolent. "Oh, well, you'll make a good pair, I'm sure."

"Thanks for practically nothing," said

Susan curtly, and went on back to her own room.

She was packing her bag when, a few minutes later, Elizabeth tapped at the door and came in.

"You're leaving, Miss Merrill?" she asked anxiously.

"Not until after the funeral in the morning, Elizabeth," Susan answered.

"I'm glad of that," sighed Elizabeth, her eyes red with weeping. "Sandy and me will be leaving, too, as soon as everything is over. I'm worried about Stepp, Miss Merrill. He's gone completely to pieces. He's got hold of some whiskey and he's really tying one on, as Sandy calls it."

Susan hesitated and then said quietly, "I don't think we ought to scold him for that, Elizabeth. He was closer to Mr. Cantrell than anybody else, and I suppose he feels the whole bottom has dropped out of his world. Where is he?"

"Sandy's got him stashed away in our apartment over the garage and has put him to bed."

"Good! Then let's just leave him there until he gets himself under control," suggested Susan. "There's nothing I could do for him except pour black coffee down him; and the whiskey is a sort of sedative. He'll come out of it all right, I'm sure. Does he ever get violent when he's drinking?"

Elizabeth shook her head. "No, he just goes to sleep and wakes up with an awful hang-over," she answered, and sighed deeply. "I guess maybe you're right, miss. Best just to leave him alone and let him sleep it off. I'm sure glad you're going to be here tomorrow. Seems like it's only right that there should be somebody at the funeral to grieve for him because they loved him, don't it?"

"It does, indeed, Elizabeth. And there will also be you and Sandy and Maisie. And Stepp will be all right by then. And there's Dr. Murdock," Susan told her gently.

"*That* one," said Elizabeth, and Susan knew by her tone that she meant Joyce, "was talking about having a private funeral; nobody but themselves. I sure put a stop to that, but *fast!*"

Startled, Susan asked, "How, Elizabeth?"

Elizabeth folded her arms across her stomach and cocked her head belligerently.

"I just told her that there was a heap of folks in these parts that had mighty good reason to love Mr. Cantrell and who wouldn't be willing just to see him shoved into a crypt without so much as paying their respects to him. And then when she talked to Mr. Lawson in Atlanta, he told her that there were instructions in the will about how the chief wanted his funeral to be held. She was plenty mad about that, I can tell you. But she had to do as she was told! And high time, too."

"Well, by this time tomorrow, Elizabeth, they will be gone and so will we," Susan tried to soothe her. Then she asked, "Have they said anything about staying on here after the will is read? The place will belong to them, of course."

"Them stay here? In a pig's eye they

would!" sniffed Elizabeth. "No, that one that's a lawyer is already making up an advertisement to be placed in some fancy magazine advertising the place for sale. Seems like they can't get out of here fast enough! And that's the way I feel about them, too."

"Where will you and Sandy and Maisie go, Elizabeth?" asked Susan as she went back to her packing.

"Oh, we haven't decided that yet," Elizabeth answered. "Several years ago the chief set up a trust fund for us that gives us a tidy income, so we can be right independent and see Maisie through her final training."

She looked out of the window toward the green sloping lawn, the handsome trees, the glimmer of sunlight on the ocean, and drew a deep sigh.

"Not that we'll ever be really happy anywhere but here," she admitted. "We've lived here so long, we sort of felt it was our home, as well as the chief's. That was the way he wanted us to feel, seemed like."

Her expression altered, as did her voice, when she asked, "Miss Merrill, you know what that one asked me before the chief had been dead three hours?"

Susan waited, and Elizabeth went on, her voice touched with anger, "She wanted Sandy and me to stay on here as caretakers until the place was sold. Said she and her brothers would spend the afternoon and evening doing an inventory on the place, and then they would hold Sandy and me responsible for everything being here and in its right place when it was sold."

Susan hesitated a moment and then said quietly, "Elizabeth, that might not be a bad idea. It would give you a chance to accustom yourself to the thought of a change and give you time really to make up your mind where you wanted to go. Why don't you think it over, at least, before you tell her you won't?"

Elizabeth hesitated, obviously finding the idea more appealing now that Susan had pointed out its advantages.

"Well, we'll think about it, I suppose,"

she agreed at last, "I'll have to talk it over with Sandy and Maisie. And I kinda worry about what's going to happen to Stepp. Of course, he's got an income, too, from a trust fund the chief established for him at the same time he gave me and Sandy ours. But Stepp's liable just to run wild with nobody to keep an eye on him —nobody that belongs to him or that he belongs to. That's a right bad feeling, Miss Merrill."

"I know it is, Elizabeth," Susan agreed. "We'll talk it over with Dr. Murdock, and maybe he can suggest something. But nothing can be done until after tomorrow."

"No, I reckon not," Elizabeth answered with a deep sigh and a mist of tears she tried hard to control. "Well, now, Miss Merrill, can I help you?"

"No, thanks a lot, Elizabeth," Susan told her, and patted her arm comfortingly. "We're going to have to learn to live without him, Elizabeth; and it isn't going to be easy. But we have to do it."

"Well, yes, sure we do," admitted Elizabeth, and added, "I'd better go get lunch started. They'll be yelling to be fed first thing you know."

12

THE small church was crowded and the scent of flowers all but overpowering, even with all the windows open and a gentle breeze blowing. Men and women in their best clothes, villagers who had known and had many reasons for admiring Gerard Cantrell, made their slow, respectful way past the casket covered with a magnificent blanket of white orchids.

The services were brief, and had a simplicity and a reverence that brought tears to Susan's eyes. Dr. Murdock, beside her in the pew, looked down at her with a tender smile and enfolded her hand in his.

When at last it was all over and they were once more beside the cars, a tall, well-set-up man with a thick mane of iron-gray hair above a pleasantly homely, sun-bronzed face came up to Susan and

Dr. Murdock, extending his hand with a friendly smile.

"You're Dr. Murdock, of course," he said pleasantly. "I'm John Lawson, Mr. Cantrell's attorney."

"I'm delighted to meet you," said Dr. Murdock, and shook hands. "This is Miss Merrill, who was Mr. Cantrell's nurse."

"Ah, yes, I remember meeting you at the hospital the day I came to see Gerard about his will," said Mr. Lawson. "I never forget a pretty girl."

"That's very kind of you, Mr. Lawson," Susan thanked him politely.

Elizabeth and Sandy were already in the station wagon, and Joyce, David and Grady stood beside it, watching Mr. Lawson chatting with Susan and Dr. Murdock.

"We're waiting, Mr. Lawson," Joyce called peremptorily.

Mr. Lawson's brows went up ever so slightly, and his grin invited Dr. Murdock and Susan to share his amusement.

"You're coming to the Cedars for the reading of the will, aren't you, Doctor?" he suggested.

"I think not, thanks."

"I'm sorry, but I'm afraid I'll have to insist, Doctor," said Mr. Lawson with a quiet authority that made Susan and Dr. Murdock stare at him. "Mr. Cantrell especially wished you both to be there. Didn't he tell you?"

"Well, no, as a matter of fact he never hinted at any such thing," Dr. Murdock answered, obviously surprised.

"It will be to your advantage to be there, Doctor," said Mr. Lawson, and chuckled. "Gerard and I had quite a laugh about it. He said the only thing he would really mind would be not seeing their faces when the will is read. So you'd better come along."

He grinned at them and walked to the station-wagon where the others were waiting, climbed in, and the station-wagon drove away from the cemetery at what Sandy obviously considered a sufficiently decorous pace.

Susan looked at Dr. Murdock's scowling face and said unsteadily, "Darling, I'm scared!"

"Now what in blazes are you afraid of?" he demanded as he helped her into the car and stood for a moment beside it.

"But he wouldn't—oh, Scott, he *wouldn't*, would he? Not when I told him I didn't want him to. I *begged* him not to. Oh, Scott, if he did, in spite of me—" She was stammering now, her face quite white beneath the delicate peach-bloom of the suntan she had acquired.

"Hey, wait a minute! You're gibbering, darling, and I haven't the faintest notion what's got you upset," he protested.

Swiftly, her voice shaking, she told him of that afternoon in Mr. Cantrell's room when she had started to read the paper to him and he had threatened to call his lawyer and have his will changed to make *her* his heir.

"But I told him I didn't want him to, and what terrible things would happen to me, because they'd tear me to bits," she finished. Her voice was shaking, and her hand clung to his so tightly that the pressure made him wince. "He wouldn't, not when he knew I didn't want him to, now would he?"

"Of course he wouldn't, darling. You knew him well enough to know he wouldn't for worlds do anything that would distress or upset you," Dr. Murdock soothed her, his brows drawn together in a puzzled scowl. "And anyway, Lawson said that the will was changed at the hospital before you came to the Cedars. You were just another nurse at the hospital. True, you were his special nurse, and I'm sure he felt he owed you a lot for taking such good care of him, but not enough to do something for his own pleasure that would upset you."

He mopped her eyes with his handkerchief, grinned warmly at her and said, "Now stop getting yourself all wrought up and let's get going."

As they drove, he went on after a moment's thought, "You and I have a lot of plans to make, so right after we leave the Cedars drive back with me to the office and we'll plan. OK by you?"

She smiled up at him, dewy-eyed, and said huskily, "Very OK by me, darling. And thanks."

"Thanks? For what?" he wondered aloud.

"For being you," she drawled, and snuggled closer to him as the car went singing up the road it knew so well because it had traveled it so often.

The station-wagon stood in the drive as they rolled up behind it, but Elizabeth and Sandy were not in sight. They must be preparing lunch, Susan told herself as she got out of the car and walked beside Dr. Murdock into the house.

From the living room she could hear Joyce's voice, touched with anger, even a bit shrill, which meant she was not bothering to be charming.

"But if we are going to leave this afternoon, Mr. Lawson, I can't see why the reading of the will should be delayed until after lunch," she was saying irritably.

"Elizabeth will take some little time to get lunch ready."

"There will be plenty of time for the reading of the will after lunch, Mrs. Gilbert." John Lawson's voice was smoothly pleasant. "And I must confess I never liked to read wills on an empty stomach. I have to admit I'm hungry!"

Sandy came along the corridor toward the door of the living room, grinned at Susan and Dr. Murdock, and in the library doorway said, "Lunch is served."

"Well," Joyce said in that same irritable tone, "it's about time. Come along, everybody."

As they reached the door of the dining room, Maisie and the child Barbie were just entering from the back terrace. Barbie, in a damp bathing suit that was covered with sand, a sand pail and shovel in one hand, her other hand held close in Maisie's, glowered at her mother. Her baby face was a small replica of her mother's, and her manner was so like her mother's that Susan was almost startled.

"Good heavens, Barbie, you look like

a ragamuffin. Where have you been?" demanded Joyce.

Barbie drew closer to Maisie, scowling at her mother.

"Maisie took me to the beach and I built a castle," Barbie answered. "But it got washed away. Maisie says I can build another after lunch."

"After lunch we will be leaving the Cedars," Joyce told the child in a voice touched with triumph. "Clean her up, Maisie, and get her dressed. I suppose you'd better feed her, too."

Without waiting for an answer, as though it were inconceivable to her that there could be one, Joyce led the way into the dining room. As they were seating themselves, she looked with insolent surprise at Dr. Murdock and Susan.

"Oh, are you staying for lunch?" she demanded.

Mr. Lawson said smoothly, "At my request, Mrs. Gilbert. I wanted them here for the reading of the will."

Joyce and her brothers stared at him and then at each other. After a moment

Joyce lifted her shoulders in a slight shrug of dismissal and said coldy, "I suppose we should have realized that Uncle Gerry would want to reward them for their care of him with a small legacy."

"I think so," said Mr. Lawson, and turned to Dr. Murdock with a pleasant comment on the beauty of the island and especially of the Cedars.

Between them they managed some semblance of a conversation while the others ate steadily, as if they were anxious to get this preliminary over and done with as quickly as possible.

When at last they rose from the table and went back to the living room, Mr. Lawson took his place beside a coffee table, opened his briefcase and drew out a blue-coated legal document at the sight of which the eyes of Gerard Cantrell's relatives glistened with avarice.

Mr. Lawson cleared his throat and began reading. First came a list of bequests and donations to various charities that had held Gerard's interest for years, to which the three listened impatiently. Then finally Mr. Lawson reached the part of the will for which they were all straining forward.

He looked up, his eyes lingering for a moment on Joyce's face, passing on to Grady's and then to David's before they dropped once more to the document in his hand.

"'Since,'" he read without expression, "'I have provided adequately for my niece, Joyce Barford Gilbert, my nephews, David and Grady Barford, in the manner that seemed best to me, by irrevocable trust funds by which they enjoy a comfortable way of life, I therefore feel that the residue of my estate, both real and personal, should go to someone who will be able to make such use of it as will benefit others. I wish the residue of my estate, including my beloved home, the Cedars, to go to my good friend Scott Murdock, MD, for whatever use he wishes to make of it.'"

There was a moment of stunned silence. Scott Murdock was as stunned, as incredulous as the others, and Susan watched him anxiously, grateful that her own name had not appeared in the will.

Mr. Lawson looked up, his expressionless glance crossing the three stunned faces, and then he went on, "There is, of course, a codicil concerning the Blakes and the man called Stepp. They are to have a life estate in the Cedars and have been provided with a trust fund that will give them a comfortable living."

He folded the document and smiled pleasantly as he thrust it back into his briefcase. Then he stood up and said politely, "I think that is all."

David was on his feet, eyes blazing, his fists clenched.

"We'll contest the will," he snarled.

Mr. Lawson eyed him coolly, smiling faintly.

"That's your privilege of course, Barford," he said smoothly. "But as an attorney I think you know that it will be an expensive and long-drawn-out business and will have no effect on the will at all. My firm does not draw up wills with loopholes. Contest if you like, however."

"We'll contest, and we'll also file suit against this quack!" David shouted. "He and that nurse have been conspiring, using pressure on my uncle—"

"Don't talk like a fool, Barford," snapped Mr. Lawson. "This will was drawn up while your uncle was in the hospital in Atlanta, long before he came here for Dr. Murdock's treatment."

"Then he was of unsound mind," Joyce cried out.

"You'd have quite a chore proving that, Mrs. Gilbert," said Mr. Lawson. "Two of the doctors at the hospital, friends of mine and of your uncle's, witnessed the signature of the will and will be happy to testify to the fact that his mind was quite sound and that he was in full possession of all his faculties when it was drawn up."

The three turned on Dr. Murdock, and Susan shivered at the fury and the hatred in their eyes.

"You knew about this will," David accused him furiously. "That's why you used that mystery drug. You knew it would take him off before we had time to

218

convince him we should be his legal heirs. I'll file suit against you for malpractice and I'll make it stick. You wait and see!"

"You'll probably try," said Dr. Murdock, and his tone was cool, undisturbed. "I can't stop you from filing the suit."

"You bet you can't! Nobody can! You've taken advantage of my uncle and used him for a guinea pig, and that's against the law! I'll have your license to practice; you'll be kicked out of the medical profession. And you should be. A man who would deliberately experiment on a man who had only a short time to live—"

"And without the consent or approval of his family," Joyce screamed.

Mr. Lawson was looking on, listening, obviously amused by the whole scene.

"The consent of the family to the use of the drug was not necessary, since the patient himself gave it," Dr. Murdock pointed out.

"Of course! You *would* persuade him to risk something dangerous, something that had never been tried on human beings before," blazed Joyce.

"But it has been, both here and abroad," Dr. Murdock pointed out in that quiet voice that made Susan stare at him in startled admiration. "And there has been a record of remission of the disease. I admit the patients who have been helped were younger than Mr. Cantrell, and I told him he would have only a fifty-fifty chance."

"So you gave him the drug, after promising that it would save him, and he died!" David said savagely. "How do we know he might not have lived for years without the drug?"

"The autopsy findings prove that he would not; that he had lived beyond the time the hospital thought he would have. I am convinced the drug is responsible for that."

"Oh, sure, that's what you'd say!" sneered Joyce. "You and that girl friend of yours! You must have been pretty upset when the boys and I arrived and interfered with your little scheme."

"Oh," asked Dr. Murdock, and though his tone was polite, his eyes were glacial, "did you interfere? I wasn't aware of that."

"No, you took good care to see to it that we knew nothing of what was going on between you and this girl friend. You wouldn't even allow us in his room for more than a few minutes." Joyce was blazing-eyed.

"At his own orders," Dr. Murdock told her.

"That's what *you* say." David was grimly furious. "How do we know you aren't lying?"

Dr. Murdock studied him for a moment and then said coolly, "Come to think of it, you don't!"

"Then you admit that you kept us away from Uncle just for your own and this girl's purposes?" demanded David.

"I admit nothing except that Mr. Cantrell asked that you not be allowed free access to his room and ordered Stepp and Susan to see to it that his orders were carried out," Dr. Murdock told him flatly.

"I don't believe you!" snapped Joyce.

"That's your privilege." Dr. Murdock's tone was a pleasant drawl that did not match the anger in his eyes.

Mr. Lawson's voice intruded into the scene in a weary tone that suggested this sort of thing was by no means unusual for him.

"If we are going to make connections for that plane you people plan to catch, we'd better be leaving, hadn't we?" he suggested smoothly.

Joyce and the two men whirled on him, angry and astounded.

"You think we'd leave now?" Joyce blazed hotly.

"Not a chance!" David backed her up. "Possession is nine points of the law, as we both know, Lawson. We are staying right here for the present. If anybody is leaving, it will be this quack doctor and his girl friend."

John Lawson met his angry eyes and his blazing rage with a slight smile.

"But there is no question as to who is the owner of the Cedars, Mr. Barford," he drawled, and touched his brief case significantly. "I shall file this will for probate the first thing in the morning, and I'm sure Dr. Murdock will be able to come up to Atlanta for a day or so for the signing of the necessary papers that will install him as the new owner, with all the rights and appurtenances thereto!"

"You go ahead and file for probate," said David harshly, "while I go in town and swear out a warrant for his arrest on a charge of malpractice."

"That would be a very foolish thing to do, Barford," Mr. Lawson argued reasonably. "You could never make the charge stick."

"Well, I could keep him in hot water for a while; create a scandal; make people wonder if they really want him as their doctor; and maybe have the medical society suspend or revoke his license."

"Well, of course, if you don't mind making a fool of yourself," Mr. Lawson said dryly. "I shouldn't think it would do your career much good to get involved in such a case."

"Suppose you let me worry about my career," sneered David. "One-third of three million dollars would take care of any damage I might suffer through such a suit, I assure you."

Mr. Lawson's eyebrows went up slightly.

"Three million dollars?" he repeated. "Oh, come now, Barford, I'm afraid you've been misinformed."

David demanded, "You mean it's more?"

"I mean it's considerably less," Mr. Lawson said. "After all, the establishment of trust funds for yourself, your brother and sister, for the Blakes and Stepp, as well as the various charity bequests and legacies, amount to quite a bit. The residue is a little less than one million, after taxes."

David and the other two exchanged startled, angry glances.

"So he's been throwing his money around, has he?" David growled.

"I'm afraid so. Trust funds are expensive when they provide an income of something over twenty thousand a year, each," Mr. Lawson pointed out. "Those for the Blakes and Stepp provide only ten thousand a year each; but even trust funds like that aren't bought for nickels and dimes."

The three Barfords looked at each other, and Susan felt a twinge of unwilling pity for their bitter disappointment.

After a moment David said grimly, "Well, even that, with what we can get for the Cedars, is worth a fight. And believe me, we're going to fight! This quack is going to be driven out of the field of medicine."

Susan heard an angry voice she scarcely recognized as her own saying hotly, "You stop calling him a quack doctor, ambulance-chasing jack-leg!"

They had all but forgotten her presence, and now, as her angry voice cut into the scene, they all turned startled eyes on her. But Susan held her ground for a moment, giving them back their anger.

"I think you are three of the lowest forms of life that ever crawled!" Her voice was shaking and her hands were clenched so tightly that the nails bit into her palms, as her eyes raked them. "You're like vultures, hovering over a dying animal, waiting for the last breath to leave! You had no right to the Cedars or anything else Mr. Cantrell left. All you wanted from him was money and money and more money; and he gave it to you without question, without hesitation. Eventually you looked on him as nothing more than a money machine. And now that you've found he had emotions and feelings and people who loved him for himself, not because he was rich, you're busily trying to keep his wishes from being carried out."

She drew a long hard breath and rushed on, "I've got news for you! A few days after you came here, Mr. Cantrell threatened to call his lawyer to come down so he could change his will and leave everything he had to *me!*"

"Why, you lying little hussy!" cried Joyce furiously.

"I'm not lying. He wanted to! But I wouldn't let him!"

"Oh, don't take us for fools! You'd have let him like a shot if you thought you could have got away with it," sneered Joyce. "Tell me, was that when he told you he had made a will leaving everything to your precious quack? So you decided that would be better all around, because you and the quack were in cahoots anyway?"

Susan took a threatening step toward her, one fist clenched tightly.

"You call him a quack just one more time!" she threatened.

"He *is* a quack and we both know it—" Joyce began.

Susan's hand flew out, and with a resounding smack she struck Joyce full in the face. There was a moment of stunned silence, in which the men stared at the two women.

The imprint of Susan's hand showed on Joyce's face and Susan, with a sudden shocked realization of what she had done, looked swiftly about the group, shamed color pouring into her face, before she turned and ran out of the room, across the terrace and down to the beach. There, she dropped on a palm log that was half-bedded in the sand and sat, her face hidden in her hands, her shoulders shaking with convulsive weeping.

She was still sobbing when Dr. Murdock, a gleam of mirth in his eyes, found her and dropped down beside her, his arm drawing her close to him, holding her as she burrowed her face into his shoulder.

"Oh, Scott, Scott, how could I have done such a thing? I'm so ashamed!" she wailed.

"Well, don't be!" he consoled her, and she caught the thread of laughter in his voice even as he strove to comfort her. "Lawson and I enjoyed it tremendously. Both of us had been wanting to do it, but gents aren't supposed to sock ladies!"

"Well, she's no lady and I don't suppose I am, either, but oh, darling, I couldn't just stand there and let her go on calling you a *quack!*"

"Well, maybe they'll give us adjoining cells," Dr. Murdock comforted her.

Susan jerked away from him and stared at him, wide-eyed.

"Adjoining cells?" she repeated, bewildered.

"Oh, yes, we're both going to be arrested, you know," he assured her. "I'm to be charged with malpractice and undue influence on a patient to get him to change his will; and you're to be charged with assault and battery."

"Scott, you can't mean that!" she gasped.

"You think not?" Dr. Murdock's tone was bitter. "They've gone to the village. Sandy is to drive Mr. Lawson to the airport, and he is to drop them off at the sheriff's office where they are going to swear out warrants demanding our arrest."

Susan stared at him for a long, dazed

moment and then said grimly, "Now I'm not a bit ashamed of slugging her. I only wish I'd hit her harder!"

And Dr. Murdock grinned as he drew her back into his arm and they sat looking out over the long, slow breakers that crept in and smashed on the beach just beyond their feet.

13

THEY were still there perhaps an hour later, though neither of them had given much thought to the passing of time, when a stout, middle-aged man in khaki shirt and trousers, a wide-brimmed hat pushed back from his ruddy, perspiring face, came down from the house. A younger man, smart-looking in his uniform, walked a pace or two behind him.

Dr. Murdock and Susan stood up, hand in hand, waiting as Sheriff Elsas approached. Dr. Murdock approached the man with outstretched hand and a friendly grin.

"Hello, Sheriff; hi, Jud," Dr. Murdock greeted them as friends. "I don't believe you've met Miss Merrill."

"Howdy, Miss Merrill," said the sheriff, and added, "This is just about the craziest thing I ever heard of in my life.

It just don't make no kind of sense at all."

Dr. Murdock laughed. "Did you bring the handcuffs, Sheriff? We'll go quietly, won't we, honey?"

Susan was unable to take so light a view of the matter and watched the sheriff uneasily.

"You admit you clouted this old girl, Miss Merrill?" asked the sheriff awkwardly.

Susan's head went up.

"I certainly did, Sheriff. She kept calling Scott—I mean Dr. Murdock—a quack doctor, and—well, I smacked her, *hard!*"

The sheriff beamed at her.

"Well, good for you, miss. I can imagine just how you felt," he said frankly. "Reckon it had been me I'd have done the same, or worse. Can't remember when I ever run into people I didn't like as much as I don't like those three. Who the blazes are they, anyway?"

"Mr. Cantrell's niece and nephews,

from New York," Dr. Murdock answered.

"Oh, tourists, eh? I might have known. About the only trouble we ever have here on the island is from tourists. Island folk get along fine with each other. Oh, there's a shootin' scrape now and then; couple of fishermen get a big haul and celebrate at the tavern and get into a fight and all their friends join in. But that's easy to handle. We just slap 'em in the cooler overnight and next day when they've slept it off they are good friends again and everything's fine. But tourists! *Phooey!*"

Dr. Murdock nodded, and there was a twinkle in his eyes.

"I know what you mean, Sheriff," he answered, and waited.

Sheriff Elsas pushed his broad-brimmed hat back on his head, scraped his thumb over his jaw and said unhappily, "Reckon there's nothing I can do, Doc, but take you and the little lady into custody, much as I hate to do it."

"Don't be a chump, Hank. Don't you suppose I know you have to do that? You couldn't refuse to serve warrants that have been duly sworn to and all that. And believe me, they won't let you rest until they know that you have placed us under arrest. Shall we get going?"

As they walked up the beach together, Susan and Dr. Murdock still hand in hand, Dr. Murdock asked conversationally, "How's the little girl, Sheriff? Foot healing properly?"

The sheriff looked at him in surprise.

"Well, sure, Doc. You said it would, and it is. Why, she can walk on it good as ever."

"Wonderful!" said Dr. Murdock and looked down at Susan. "Sheriff Elsas has a beautiful little ten-year-old daughter who stepped on a piece of broken bottle. Got a very bad cut; there was some slight infection and a considerable loss of blood. But you heard him say she's fine now. That's wonderful, isn't it?"

Susan met the sheriff's eyes and asked, "Do you wonder I won't stand by and let people call him a quack?"

"No, ma'am, I sure don't!" There was

a deep vigor and emphasis in the sheriff's tone as they climbed up from the beach to the drive where a dusty dark-green sedan, with the sheriff's official plates attached, was parked behind Dr. Murdock's car.

Elizabeth and Sandy were in the drive and came forward as they reached the top of the path.

"Hank Elsas, what kind of a fool are you making of yourself?" Elizabeth demanded sharply. "Sandy here's telling me some cockeyed story about you being here to arrest Doctor and Miss Merrill. I never heard anything so crazy in my life."

"Now, now, Elizabeth," Sheriff Elsas protested unhappily, "I'm just doing what I was sworn to do: take into custody anybody a warrant has been sworn out for. You know I wouldn't do anything to Doc I didn't *have* to do!"

"Well, you'd better not!" Elizabeth said hotly, and looked at Susan accusingly. "I *told* you a little rat poison in their vittles would be a mighty fine idea."

"Oh, come now, Elizabeth!" Dr.

Murdock laughed. "It's not as bad as all that. The Barfords feel I've robbed them, and naturally they want protection."

"Protection! I'd like to protect 'em by putting a couple of rattlesnakes in their beds!" snapped Elizabeth.

"Where are the Barfords, Sandy?" asked Dr. Murdock.

"Oh, I dropped 'em off in the village, Doc," said Sandy, and grinned. "Thought walking back might be good for 'em. Give 'em a chance to cool off a bit. And mad as they were last I saw of 'em, I'd say that was a right good idea."

"Sandy and me will be gone when they get back here!" Elizabeth announced grimly. "That's if they have the nerve to come back."

"Oh, they will, Elizabeth, they will!" Susan said. "Sandy, will you get my bags and bring them out?"

"You're leaving for good, Miss Merrill?" protested Sandy.

Susan glanced at the sheriff and said awkwardly, "I'm being arrested, Sandy. And if I have to stay in jail until I apologize for socking Joyce Gilbert, I'll be an old, old woman before I hear the cell door click to let me out."

"Aw, now, miss," protested Sheriff Elsas, deeply embarrassed and very unhappy. "You ought to know we haven't got a jail cell in the village suitable for a lady, or for a man like Doc, either. All I have to do is take you down, book you and let you go, on your own assurance you will be available when the time for the trial is set."

"Then you won't need your luggage, miss," said Elizabeth warmly. "I'm right glad you'll be coming back here. I sure wouldn't want to be here with nobody around but them!"

"Guess we'd best be going, Doc," said the sheriff, and he and his deputy walked to the green sedan. "You can follow us or we'll follow you; makes no difference."

Dr. Murdock nodded as he helped Susan into his car and drove off after the green sedan. Behind them, Sandy and Elizabeth stood watching until both cars vanished.

Susan looked uneasily at Dr. Murdock as he drove. There was no longer any pretense of lightness about him. His jaw was set and hard and his eyes were on the road ahead.

"Darling?" she said at last, her voice soft, uncertain.

He glanced down at her and smiled tenderly. "There's nothing to worry about, honey."

"A suit for malpractice, Scott? A suit like that never did any doctor any good, and we both know it," she told him swiftly, sitting erect, her eyes flashing. "Oh, it's all very well for you to be gay and nonchalant about it. But, darling, I'm *scared!*"

"Look, honey, do you think I'm really amused about this malpractice suit? Of course I know it's damaging to a doctor's reputation, especially if there is a large inheritance involved. But I'm completely in the clear. Mr. Lawson has offered to help. A friend of his is an expert in suits of this kind. He will testify himself, so he can't be the defense attorney. And I'm sure Dr. Willard and Dr. Hudson will also testify in my defense. Who knows? It might even give me some good publicity!" He tried very hard to make his voice light and amusing, but he was by no means successful, and Susan looked up at him, her heart in her eyes.

"As if you needed any publicity!" she protested loyally and added impulsively, "Scott darling, we don't need the inheritance. That's what they are after. Why don't we give it to them?"

"And go against everything we both know Mr. Cantrell wanted? How can you suggest such a thing?" There was more than a hint of anger in his voice.

"Well, what are we going to do with it?" she asked quietly.

"You don't like the Cedars?"

"Oh, don't be silly. I adore the place. But it's much too big for just us."

"And they want to sell it: turn it into a lodge or a hotel or something of the sort. So we'll keep it and turn it into a nursing home for convalescents."

She sat up and stared at him, wide-eyed.

"Why, Scott, that's a wonderful idea!" she gasped.

"I think so," he told her, smiling. "I've thought so for a long time. There is a very real need in this area for such a place. When a patient no longer needs the expert medical attention and nursing care of a hospital, but is not quite strong enough to go home, a convalescent home is the perfect solution. With the crowded conditions of all the hospitals in this area, such a place as the Cedars would be an answer to any hospital administrator's prayers."

"Oh, yes! Wouldn't it just!" she agreed with shining eyes.

Ahead of them the sheriff's green sedan had turned in at the parking space beside the city hall that also housed the sheriff's office, the jail and the offices the village administration required.

Dr. Murdock followed the sheriff's car. As he and Susan got out of his car, Sheriff Elsas came to meet them, smiling as he thrust his hat back from his perspiring forehead.

"Some friends of yours inside, Doc, in my office. Right this way." He led the way through a side entrance and into his own small, shabbily furnished office. "Well, here he is, folks."

Three men stood up, and Dr. Murdock's eyes took them in with instant recognition. They were the village's three most influential citizens: Jim Gordon, who ran the bank; Merv Jenkins, who owned and operated the village's biggest fishing fleet; and elderly, dignified Jerome Marshall, owner of the village's one department store.

There were friendly greetings, and Dr. Murdock introduced Susan, who was warmly welcomed by the three men. It was Jim Gordon, as befitted his position as the town's most respected citizen, who did the talking.

"This is an outrage, Scott, the whole silly, messy business," he began. "The moment we heard about it we came down to see what could be done about making bond for you. And the lady, too, of course."

"That's very good of you, Jim. I appreciate it very much," said Dr. Murdock sincerely.

"Good of me, after what you've done for the sick and ailing in this village? There's not much the village, man, woman or child, wouldn't do if you needed it," Jim Gordon answered, and added, with a faint quirk of his mouth, "I think it would be a very good idea if those tourists left the Cedars before dark. If word of this gets around, some of our more easily aroused citizens may take things into their own hands and run 'em out."

"Now see here, Jim, don't you go spreading no such talk around, with nobody but Bill and me to preserve law and order around here," protested Sheriff Elsas uneasily.

"Oh, you could probably find a few of the less easily aroused citizenry to act as special deputies; only I wouldn't count on it," said Jim firmly, and added, "Well,

242

get on with it, man. What bail are you setting?"

"Now you know danged good and well, Jim, I have nothing to do with that." Sheriff Elsas was annoyed. "That'll be up to the Justice of the Peace when he's arraigned. And that can't be before tomorrow or next day. He's holding court up at Pine Valley."

Jim demanded sharply, while the others echoed his words with angry looks, "Are you trying to tell me that you're going to lock Dr. Murdock and this lady up until Justice Foreman can get back?"

"Now, keep your shirt on, Jim!" Sheriff Elsas cut in sharply, "you know danged well I'm not going to do no such thing. They can go home any time they want to. And they don't have to make bond to do it, either. They only have to tell me they'll be here as soon as Curt Foreman gets back."

"Well, I just wanted to be sure."

"You got no call to want to be sure about a thing like that!" barked the sheriff. "I owe Doc as much as you do;

243

just about everybody in this village owes him a heap. And I don't mean just money, either; though I bet if he could collect just about fifty percent of the bills owing him, he'd be in mighty good shape financially. Ain't that right, Doc?"

Dr. Murdock laughed. "Well, we won't go into that at the moment," he answered cautiously, and went on, "I don't like to mention this, but I am pretty late for my afternoon office hours, so if it's all right with you gentlemen, may I drop in and see if any patients are willing to trust me, now that it's no doubt generally known that I'm being accused of incompetence?"

"Don't you worry about that, Scott," said Jim Gordon. "When I came back to the clinic an hour ago, the place was jammed and they were spilling over onto the lawn. Guess you know how fast the grapevine works down here without me trying to tell you."

"I do, indeed," said Dr. Murdock. "Well, thanks a lot, gentlemen. And, Hank, you know where to find me when I'm wanted."

"Sure do, Doc," Sheriff Elsas agreed, and glanced at Susan. "You going back to the Cedars, miss, while them Barfords are there?"

Susan hesitated for just a moment, then tilted her chin at a defiant angle and said coolly, "Why, yes, Sheriff, I am, if there is no objection from your office."

"None at all, miss, none at all. But— well, Doc, you reckon it will be safe for her there, after the way those three cut up?"

Dr. Murdock looked down at Susan and grinned.

"You mean safe for *them* or safe for *her?*" he drawled.

Color poured into Susan's face, but she went on meeting his eyes squarely.

"Oh, I won't hit her again, I promise," she said sweetly. "And I might be able to keep Elizabeth from sprinkling poison on their food. She's mentioned doing it several times, and I've managed to talk her out of it."

"That's too bad," said Jim Gordon, and smiled warmly at her. "I'm glad

245

you're going to be staying on awhile, Miss Merrill. Planning on working with Scott? He needs a nurse badly in his clinic, I happen to know."

Susan looked merrily up at Dr. Murdock and said, "Oh, I'm planning to stay as long as he wants me to. I'm going to marry him the minute this is over with."

"Well, now, that's mighty good news!" said Jim, and the other men agreed. "A lady like you will be a big asset to the village. We could use more such ladies."

"Sorry, she's unique. There's only one of her, and we're going to keep her here," said Dr. Murdock.

"You'd be a fool not to, Doc," Sheriff Elsas told him, grinning.

"And don't I know it!" Dr. Murdock agreed with such vigor that Susan beamed and her color deepened.

Goodbyes were said, thanks offered and rejected, and Susan and Dr. Murdock went out to where his car was waiting. He sat for a moment behind the wheel, and then he looked down at Susan and grinned warmly.

"You know something? You're quite a girl!"

"Well, thanks, Doctor! You're not so bad yourself!"

"If there is anything I do like, it's enthusiasm, sheer, unrestrained enthusiasm," he drawled, "such as the tone in which you say, 'You're not so bad yourself.' I'm overcome!"

"Would you really like to know what I think of you?" she asked very softly. "I think you are wonderful—handsome, gifted, dedicated, hard-working—and I'm the luckiest girl in the world to have snagged you for my own."

"Oh, *you* snagged *me*, did you? I thought all the time I was pursuing you!" he protested.

"Oh, men are always supposed to think that. It's *part of* our feminine wiles, you see. We see someone we think is good husband material and we start stalking him," she assured him. "Of course we have to do it cautiously, because a man who is good husband material is one of the wildest creatures anybody ever tried to hunt."

He was staring at her now, scowling slightly, obviously shaken a trifle.

"So that's the way it's done!" he murmured at last.

"That's the way it's done," she assured him, completely unabashed.

They sat for a moment, wrapped in the warm glow of their mutual love. Then his scowl deepened and he became completely serious.

"This is going to develop into a very unpleasant business before it's finished, honey," he told her grimly. "And the best thing for you is to go back to Atlanta and stay there until it's all settled."

Susan stared at him, outraged.

"And you think there is any likelihood of my doing that?"

He studied her for a moment and said quietly, "I truly wish you would, darling."

"I'm sorry to go against your wishes, Scott," she told him in a voice that assured him she would not change her mind, "but that's one thing I'll never do. I'm with you, darling, now and for always, no matter what happens! So let's not discuss it any more."

14

SITTING in the clinic waiting for Scott, Susan lost track of time. Held in a lovely dream of the future, there on the island, with Dr. Murdock and these people who so obviously loved and trusted him, she was unaware of passing cars until one stopped with a screeching of brakes and then turned into the short drive.

Startled, she sat erect and recognized the station wagon from the Cedars, with Sandy at the wheel and Elizabeth and Maisie on the front seat beside him. Stowed in the back were various cartons and suitcases and boxes.

Elizabeth, grinning, leaned out of the car and called to Susan, who came swiftly to stand beside the station wagon, looking at the three.

"Miss Susan, it would have done your heart good to see that gang when we told 'em they was on their own because we was leaving," Elizabeth boasted happily. "They're so danged sure the Cedars is going to belong to 'em when they get through accusing Doc of all the crimes in the book, so let 'em find out what it's like to live there all by theirselves without any transportation."

"But, Elizabeth—" Susan, startled, stared from one grinning face to the other.

"Sandy and me, we're going to visit my sister in Florida," announced Elizabeth happily. "Maisie, she's going to stop off in Jacksonville to see a friend. And Stepp took the big car over to the mainland this morning. Soon as the funeral was over, he lit out. So there's nothing at the Cedars that them folks can use to get around in, unless they want to walk to the village. It's less than a mile along the beach, and the exercise will do 'em good."

Susan said, "But, Elizabeth, you can't just abandon them there."

"Oh, can't we? We already have!" Elizabeth insisted, and obviously rejoiced at the fact. "I sure wish you could have been there to see it. Believe me, when they come in, mad as hornets because Sandy hadn't waited for them and they'd had to pay a fellow at the filling station to drive 'em out, we was all getting our stuff loaded. Barbie was bawling her head off because Maisie was leaving."

"I hated to do it, Miss Susan, but after all—" Maisie began awkwardly.

"After all, we wasn't about to go off and leave you there," Elizabeth cut in firmly. "It's the Gilbert woman's job to look after her own kid. Not that she does an all-fired good job of it, but that's not my affair, nor yet is it Maisie's. No, way I look at it, Miss Susan, it's high time that gang found out they can't ride rough-shod over everybody in the whole wide world. Imagine swearing out a warrant for Doc, and one for you, because you done something I've wanted to do ever since the first time I laid eyes on 'em!"

Susan said earnestly, "Look, you three! You'll be needed to testify when Scott's case comes up for trial. You, Sandy, and

Stepp witnessed the agreement Mr. Cantrell signed to allow the experimental drug to be used and your evidence will be very important. And, Elizabeth, you will probably be called, too. Oh, don't you see? You've simply got to be here when the case comes up."

The three exchanged swift, troubled glances and Sandy cleared his throat and asked, "How soon you reckon that will be, miss?"

Susan made a little despairing gesture.

"Oh, Sandy, I don't know! He hasn't even been arraigned yet. The Justice of the Peace is holding court somewhere else, and Mr. Gordon said he wouldn't be back until tomorrow some time," she answered.

"Well, court don't set until the first week in September, miss," Sandy told her. "And that's a month, six weeks off."

"We won't be far away, Miss Susan," Elizabeth assured Susan earnestly. "Not more'n a day's drive, way Sandy drives when he's in a hurry. All you got to do is send us a telegram. Here's the address

253

wrote down on this piece of paper, and there's a telephone number alongside it. So you just telephone or telegraph us when you want us and we'll be right here."

"What about Stepp? Do you know where he will be?" asked Susan, slightly comforted by the promise.

The three exchanged troubled glances, and Elizabeth shook her head.

"Well, now I couldn't rightly say about that," she admitted. "All I know is, he was going to put the big car in the garage at the mainland and leave word Dr. Murdock could get it any time he wanted it. But Stepp—well, I dunno. He's lost without the chief, and no telling where he might wind up."

"But, Elizabeth, we'll need him! We'll need him and Sandy desperately. Haven't you any idea where we can get in touch with him?" pleaded Susan.

"Well, now, miss, tell you what," suggested Sandy. "I'll stop at the garage on the mainland and see if they know where he went. He ain't had time to get very far; not if he took the car there like he said he would. There was a few little jobs he wanted done on it that he didn't think he ought to risk trying to do. Maybe we can find him, and if we do, we'll sure tell him to get in touch with Doc right away so's we'll know where to find him time comes he's needed."

"Oh, please do, Sandy!" Susan's tone thanked him warmly.

"We didn't know whether to bring your things with us or not, Miss Susan," said Elizabeth hesitantly. "You any idea where you're going? Back to Atlanta, maybe?"

Susan smiled at her. "Of course not. I'm staying right here permanently."

Elizabeth beamed at her happily and turned to Maisie and Sandy.

"See? Didn't I tell you they was crazy about each other and more'n likely would be getting married? I couldn't be more pleased, Miss Susan. I'm that happy for the both of you. Doc needs him a wife, and he couldn't do better choosing one if he had the whole world to pick from!"

Susan laughed, feeling her face warm with color.

"Now, aren't you sweet?" she answered. "Thank you, Elizabeth! And I hope we'll all be back at the Cedars soon. Scott and I have some plans for the place, but it's too soon to talk about them."

"That gang of vultures up there has some plans, too, but they don't think it's too soon to talk about what they're going to do with and *to* the Cedars as soon as they get the will busted," Elizabeth said dryly.

Susan's expression altered. "Well, we can't stop them from planning, now can we?"

"No, I reckon not," admitted Elizabeth, and added "You didn't tell us what you aim to do right now, where you're going to stay."

"Why, at the Cedars, of course," Susan answered pleasantly.

The three in the station wagon looked alarmed.

"Oh, now, Miss Susan, if you could have heard the things they was saying about you—" Elizabeth protested. "You better come on with us. My sister'll be tickled pink to have you, and she's got plenty of room."

"Thanks, Elizabeth, that's very kind," Susan answered. "But I think I'd better go back to the Cedars."

Elizabeth nodded thoughtfully, reading more into Susan's words than Susan had put there.

"Well, now, maybe you're right," she said slowly. "I don't know just how much valuable stuff they could haul off without a truck, but *them* kind, they don't stop at much! They was having a merry old time going through the desk and the chief's papers and making what the Gilbert woman called an inventory of all the things that would be removed before the place was sold. Seems like they're almighty sure they're going to get to sell it."

Susan was very still for a moment, and then she nodded at a sudden thought.

"Sounds as if a court order to prevent

257

any such activity might be a good idea," she said thoughtfully.

"Well, now, I reckon it would, but won't be nobody to issue a court order until the JP gets back from Pineville tomorrow," Sandy pointed out.

Susan frowned.

"Well, of course, if they don't have any way to haul things off, at least the place should be safe for tonight," she said.

"I reckon that's right," Sandy agreed uneasily.

"You want us to drive you back up there, miss, right now, instead of waiting for Doc?" suggested Elizabeth reluctantly.

Susan laughed. "After the way you walked out on them? I know it must have been a marvelous exit scene, Elizabeth, and I woudn't want you to spoil it by going back. No, I'll wait for Scott. You three had better get started if you've got a long drive ahead."

"Minute you think we ought to come back, you get on the telephone, Miss Susan, and we'll come faster than the speed laws allow," Elizabeth promised. "And don't you forget it!"

"I won't, Elizabeth! And thanks for everything," said Susan, and stood back as the station wagon backed into the highway and went on its way.

When Dr. Murdock came out of the clinic at last, dusk was gathering and he said anxiously as he reached the car, "Sorry, darling, I had no idea I'd be so long. Did you get tired of waiting?"

He slid beneath the wheel and looked down at her.

"Oh, I had a lot to think about," she drawled, and told him about Elizabeth, Sandy and Maisie stopping to say goodbye en route to Florida. "Stepp had already gone, but they left me an address where I can reach them when they are needed for their testimony. And they're going to try to find Stepp and let us know where we can reach him."

"Well, well," said Dr. Murdock thoughtfully, "so the Barfords are in complete possession at the Cedars. We'll

259

have to do something about that, won't we?"

"I should say we will!" Susan answered, and there was the light of battle in her eyes.

"We'd better have dinner here in the village," suggested Dr. Murdock. "Ma Ferguson's café, I'm afraid, is the best the village affords. It's certainly not the Ritz, but the food is palatable."

"I think we ought to have dinner at the Cedars so I can show you that I'm a good cook," said Susan.

Dr. Murdock looked mildly startled.

"You are going to walk right into the lion's den?" he asked.

"Why not? I'm not afraid of them! And Mr. Cantrell did want you to have the Cedars."

"You have a point," Dr. Murdock agreed, and started the car.

As they drove the scant mile and a half to the Cedars, Susan told him more of what Elizabeth had related, and by the time he parked the car in the drive his jaw was set and hard.

Lights burned all over the house, and as they came in through the front door angry voices from the direction of the kitchen reached them and loud, angry howls from Barbie laced through the voices.

Susan and Dr. Murdock walked across the big reception hall and down the corridor to the kitchen, where they paused in the doorway, for a moment unnoticed by the three people who were busy there.

"It seems to me," David was saying angrily, "that any normal woman could scramble an egg and make toast without burning it. Dammit, I'm hungry!"

Joyce, at the stove, one of Elizabeth's aprons tied over her navy blue slacks, glared at him furiously.

"Well, if you can do a better job, suppose you try it," she blazed. And to Barbie, "Shut up, you, or I'll spank you!"

"She's hungry," drawled Grady, and suddenly became aware of Dr. Murdock and Susan standing in the doorway. "Well, it's about time you were getting back, though I thought by now you'd both be locked up in a cell."

Joyce turned sharply, and her angry face, her make-up smudged by perspiration, twisted malevolently.

"Well, well, I do hope you've had dinner, because we haven't! Those outrageous Blakes have run out on us," she told them.

"I know," Susan drawled sweetly. "I saw them in the village and told them goodbye."

"Well, what are we supposed to do? They've taken both cars."

Dr. Murdock said politely, "I have my car here. I'll be glad to drive you wherever you'd like to go!"

"I'll just bet you would!" sneered David. "But you won't, Doctor. We're staying right here until after the trial."

Dr. Murdock lounged against the door frame, an amused smile in his eyes.

"I'm afraid you'll have a long wait, Mr. Barford," he drawled, his tone quite pleasant. "There won't be a session of court until the first week in September."

"*What?*" It was a Greek-chorus effect from all three of them, denoting their shocked dismay.

"Fact, I assure you," said Dr. Murdock. "Susan and I will be arraigned before the JP tomorrow, as soon as he gets back; but for trials by jury, which is what I imagine you will want—"

"You're darned right we will!" David cut in shortly.

"Then that will be the first week in September," said Dr. Murdock. "If the calendar is heavy, as it sometimes is, it may be October before a trial can be set."

The three exchanged stunned, furious glances and looked back at Dr. Murdock helplessly.

"But that's *months*," Joyce protested. "Surely something can be done before that time! I will not stay around here that long. I'd go out of my mind!"

David's eyes held Dr. Murdock's steadily.

"Perhaps we could arrange a compromise," he said, and his voice was oily with a pretense of good cheer. "After all, there

263

is quite a lot of money involved. Surely we could settle this harmoniously, out of court?"

Dr. Murdock's eyebrows went up slightly above eyes that were stony.

"Just what did you have in mind, Mr. Barford?" he asked.

David made a slight gesture.

"Oh, suppose we say fifty-fifty split, Doctor?" he suggested.

Joyce screamed a furious protest, and Grady growled sourly, "Dave, you're out of your mind!"

Dr. Murdock smiled faintly.

"The others don't seem to relish the idea any more than I do, Mr. Barford," he said calmly.

David's suave manner was wiped out by his anger.

"Now see here, Murdock," he began truculently, "what right have you got to the inheritance? We are his family; his legal heirs; his blood kin. We can break the will and take it all and fling you out of your profession on your neck! But we'll settle, giving you the Cedars and the money to be split between us—one-fourth to each of us. That's more money than you'd ever make in your whole life!"

"David, you're crazy!" Joyce cried.

"I won't agree to any such division! The money should all be ours, and the Cedars, too," Grady backed her up.

"You see?" Dr. Murdock made a negligent gesture that took in the irate two. Barbie, in her high chair, her eyes wide, was silent as she listened to the uproar about her. "I'm afraid it's no deal, Mr. Barford. Even if I agreed, and I assure you I was never farther from the idea in my life, your brother and sister wouldn't."

"You'd rather have the trial? Be held up to the public as a doctor who used undue influence on a patient who was not in possession of all his faculties to persuade him to alter his will in your favor? Exposed as someone who experimented on him with an untried drug, made a guinea pig out of him, knowing what the results would be; that he would die and you'd inherit from him?" David summed up the case, then concluded, "It's not going to be a pretty case, Dr. Murdock."

Dr. Murdock eyed him calmly.

"And of course you'll do everything you can to make it even uglier, won't you?" he drawled.

"That I will, Doctor, that I will. That's one thing you may depend on," David assured him.

Susan spoke for the first time since she had entered the room, and her tone was cool.

"We're all hungry and tired and it's been quite a day. Why don't the four of you go into the library and discuss this while I get dinner?"

Wide-eyed, Joyce stared at her.

"Can you cook?" she asked, slightly awed.

Susan smiled. "I can broil a steak and make a salad," she answered. "Would that be satisfactory?"

"Satisfactory, she asks!" Grady beamed at her. "It would be perfect!"

"Good!" said Susan. "Give me the

apron, Mrs. Gilbert, and all of you get out of the kitchen and give me room to work. I'll feed Barbie, and you can put her to bed after dinner."

Joyce surrendered the apron and followed her brothers and Dr. Murdock from the room.

Barbie was watching Susan with wary eyes. Susan smiled at her.

"Hungry, baby?" she asked lightly as she went briskly about gathering the essentials for the child's supper, bringing steaks out of the refrigerator and assembling the makings for a salad.

She put food before the child, and as Barbie began eating, Susan asked, "Would you like to hear a story, Barbie?" And at the child's enthusiastic response, she began, "Once upon a time—"

Barbie listened, fascinated, as Susan related the story, making it up as she went along, her hands busy with the preparations for the meal she was planning to serve the others. They'd eat it in the kitchen, she told herself; she wasn't going through the extra work of setting the table in the dining room. After all, they'd been preparing to eat whatever Joyce could cook in the kitchen, and the broiled steaks and salad were certainly more edible than the burned toast and eggs Joyce had been trying to serve.

When Barbie had scraped the last food from her plate and the steaks were done to sizzling perfection, Susan smiled at her.

"Would you like to run and tell Mother and the men that dinner is ready?" she suggested.

For a moment Barbie scowled at her. And then, like a ray of sunlight peeping through a cloud-heavy sky, Barbie's smile peeped through enchantingly and she slipped down from her chair. As she scampered out of the room and toward the library, Susan's eyes were wide.

Well, well, Maisie, my girl, she said to herself, you're something of a miracle worker. Maybe you were right, and all the child needed was love.

When Joyce and the others came into the kitchen, Susan's eyes went from one to the other of the four, and she felt a little glow of relief. For they were no longer screaming at each other, hurling insults; they were friendly and amicable. Susan realized that Dr. Murdock was some sort of a miracle worker himself. But then, she reminded herself loyally, hadn't she known that about him from the first? So why should she be surprised? She met his eyes for a moment and felt her face go warm with color at what she saw in his eyes.

15

IT developed, while they were eating, that an agreement satisfactory to all four had been reached and that after dinner, David would draw up a legally binding document that they would all sign and that would be delivered to John Lawson by the Barfords on their way north tomorrow.

Susan's heart gave a little leap as she realized that they would be leaving soon. It had been so unpleasant since they had been there, it was going to be a relief to know they had gone peacefully, without carrying out any of their ugly threats.

When dinner was over and they had all thanked her sincerely for a delicious meal, the three men went back to the library and Joyce picked up Barbie, who was almost asleep.

"I'll tuck her into bed, Susan, and then

I'll come back and help with the dishes," she promised as she went out.

Susan scraped the dishes, stacked them in the dishwasher and wished there was a dog to enjoy the steak bones.

Joyce came back and stood for a moment beside the table, eying Susan with a strained, uncertain look.

"Susan, I'm not much good at apologizing, because I've always been such a stinker I've never felt I owed anybody an apology," she began.

Susan laughed. "Well, please don't apologize, Mrs. Gilbert, because if you do, I'll have to, too."

Joyce looked puzzled. "But why should you apologize to me, Susan?"

Susan said pleasantly, "Well, after all, I *did* slap you! And I can't say I'm sorry, because I'd do it again, with the same provocation!"

Joyce stared at her for a moment, even as one hand went up absently to touch her cheek. And then suddenly, to Susan's amazement, she laughed, a ringing laugh of genuine amusement.

"You had a perfect right to smack me, Susan," she admitted. "I'd have smacked anybody who dared to call my beloved something he really wasn't!"

And then, as though the sound of her words had startled her, she frowned and said scarcely above her breath, "That is, I *think* I would. But do you know something, Susan? I don't think I ever loved anybody well enough to want to take up for them? That's a rather shocking thing to admit, isn't it?"

"Not shocking," Susan said quietly. "Pathetic."

Joyce stared at her.

"You're sorry for me?" she asked as though she could not quite believe it.

"I'm sorry for anybody who has never been that much in love," Susan said gently.

Joyce's eyes widened and she studied Susan for a moment as though seeing her for the first time.

"You may have a point there," she said at last, and there was a faint edge to her tone. "But anyway, I'd like to say I'm sorry for having been so beastly. Since we are leaving in the morning, with a stop-over in Atlanta to see Mr. Lawson, this may be the last chance I'll have to tell you."

Susan smiled at her forgivingly.

"It's quite all right," she answered.

Still Joyce studied her with that curi-ously appraising stare before she asked, "You were rather fond of Uncle Gerard, weren't you?"

"Very fond!" Susan answered. "Every-body in the hospital who came in contact with him liked him enormously. He was always so gentle and considerate and thoughtful and appreciative of every small thing done for him."

Joyce looked away from Susan and said awkwardly, "I never got to know him very well."

"That was your loss, Mrs. Gilbert."

Joyce's eyes turned swiftly back to her, studying her sharply.

"Well, yes, I suppose it was," she agreed unwillingly.

"Believe me, it was," Susan said

earnestly. "He was such a lovable man that you couldn't have helped loving him if you had known him better."

"Well, he always insisted on living here in this backwater place, out of reach of everything that made my life worth living. I couldn't visit him often; I'm not even sure he would have wanted me to."

"I'm sure he would," Susan said quietly, "if he had felt you came to see him because you really *wanted* to see him."

Anger flared in Joyce's eyes for a moment.

"And not just to get money out of him. Is that what you were going to say? Well, go on then and say it," she snapped and Susan smiled faintly.

"Why should I say it? You already have," she pointed out.

Joyce hesitated, and it was obvious that her chastened mood was forgotten. She was angry now, on the defensive, very aware of her own superiority to this mere nurse.

"I couldn't possibly expect you to

understand," she said loftily. "But I'm sure Uncle Gerry did. He was very proud of my social position and that of my brothers, and he must have known we couldn't maintain it by living here."

Before Susan could answer, Dr. Murdock came into the kitchen, gave both of them a mildly anxious glance and said briskly, "Mrs. Gilbert, we're ready for your signature on the agreement."

"Oh, yes, of course," said Joyce, and went toward the library.

Dr. Murdock came to Susan, drew her close and asked, "Tired, honey?"

Susan leaned against him and relaxed in the warmth of his tenderness.

"Well, there have been days at the hospital that have been more physically tiring, but less so mentally!" she said ruefully.

"I know what you mean," he responded, and kissed her lightly. "Well, it's about over now. Wait for me. I'll be right back."

He went out and along the hall to the library. A little later, Susan heard them emerge from the library, obviously all in a friendly mood as they said good night and separated.

Dr. Murdock came back to the kitchen and said lightly, "Walk me to the car?"

Susan smiled her assent, and they went out of the back door and along the terrace to where his car was parked.

"I know I should have asked you to sit in on that conference," he began, his voice faintly touched with anxiety.

"Goodness, no! I'm glad you didn't," she assured him, and added curiously, "What did you do to them to quiet them down?"

"Agreed to a four-way split of the estate, except for the Cedars," Dr. Murdock told her. "Do you think that was all right? I know it wasn't what Mr. Cantrell wanted, but after all, if I had held out against them, there would have been the malpractice suit."

"Which you'd have won, hands down!" Susan told him swifty.

"Well, yes, I know that. But it wouldn't have happened until there had been a lot of publicity. It seemed to me that it was better to pay them off than to drag the thing out through the courts, not for my sake, or for theirs—but, Susan honey, for his! Do you see what I'm getting at?"

"Of course," Susan answered swiftly. "And he would have, too. I'm sure that he knew exactly what he was doing when he made that will. But maybe if he had been here at the Cedars, maybe if he had seen them recently—oh, I don't know, darling. Somehow, I think he would be pleased that you have made the compromise."

"I hoped you'd feel like that," said Dr. Murdock, relieved. "It's the way I felt, too. They will stop off in Atlanta tomorrow and talk to Mr. Lawson."

"You're not going with them?" she protested.

"Why, no, there's no point in that! The agreement is a very imposing document. I'll talk to Mr. Lawson on the telephone in the morning and I have a strong hunch he will feel the decision to compromise is a wise one. Don't you?"

"Well, yes, I do, and I think maybe he will, too," Susan answered. "I think he'll be pleased that there is to be no long-drawn out court battle to attempt to break a will he himself drew up! He was very fond of Mr. Cantrell; they are old friends —I mean they *were!*"

She caught her breath on a small sob and for a moment hid her face against his shoulder.

"Oh, Scott, it's been such a jam-packed day. It doesn't seem possible that it was just this morning we saw him dead! We haven't even had a chance to grieve for him. Every time we realize that he's gone, something unpleasant flies up and hits us in the face and we have to cope with it."

"I know, darling. It's been quite a day!" Dr. Murdock soothed her tenderly. "What you need is a good night's rest—"

"Something you could use, too," she reminded him shakily.

There was the sound of a car in the drive, entering from the highway, and suddenly they were pinned against the brilliance of powerful headlights as the car came on.

"Now, what the devil—" Dr. Murdock wondered aloud as he reached into his car and switched on his own lights.

And then they recognized the Cadillac coming slowly up the drive, and behind it other headlights. As the Cadillac reached the doctor's car, it stopped, and Stepp leaned out from behind the wheel.

"Hi, there, Doc, I'm back," he announced unnecessarily. "Sandy and Elizabeth said you might need me if these folks stirred up a ruckus."

"Thanks, Stepp, that's very decent of you," Dr. Murdock began. But by now the station wagon had come to a halt behind the Cadillac, and Sandy leaned out to order Stepp to drive on to the garage.

"Well, keep your shirt on," Stepp called back to him. "I had to come back, you said. But I don't have to take no more of your sass."

The Cadillac rolled on to the garage,

and Sandy stopped the station wagon beside Susan and Dr. Murdock.

"Me and the old woman here—" he began, but Elizabeth cut him short.

"Who are you calling an old woman, old man?" she snapped at him. And then to Susan and Dr. Murdock, "Thing is, Sandy and me got to worrying about going off and leaving Miss Susan to stay here with these—"

"They're leaving tomorrow, Elizabeth," Dr. Murdock checked whatever epithet had trembled on her tongue. "I'm glad you're back, because we're going to need you here."

"Well, now, how'd you ever manage to get 'em to leave, Doc?" asked Sandy.

"Oh, we made a deal," Dr. Murdock admitted, and Elizabeth sniffed scornfully.

"Shame on you, Doc, for turnin' chicken!"

"Well, it was better than having Mr. Cantrell's name dragged through the courts, Elizabeth; having to prove by sworn oath that he was in sound mind

and full possession of all his faculties—
Mr. Cantrell was a man who cherished his
privacy, and he wouldn't want that kind
of thing," Dr. Murdock pointed out.

"Well, no, I don't s'pose he would,"
Elizabeth answered reluctantly, and
added, swift alarm touching her, "You're
not going to let 'em have the Cedars, are
you, Doc?"

"Of course not, Elizabeth! The Cedars
is going to be a convalescent hospital!
That's one of the reasons I said we would
need you here, you and Sandy and Stepp.
By the way, where's Maisie?"

"Oh, she's visiting a friend in Jacksonville," Elizabeth answered. "She'll come
back if she's needed, any time."

"She may be, at that," Dr. Murdock
agreed.

"Well, Sandy, we may as well get on
home and start getting unpacked," Elizabeth suggested, and turned to ask
anxiously, "Oh, did you have any dinner,
the two of you?"

"We did, indeed," Dr. Murdock
assured her.

"Don't tell me that Gilbert woman risked her nail polish cooking," Elizabeth sniffed. "What did she give you? Scrambled eggs?"

"Oh, no, we had broiled steaks done to a sizzling turn and a salad that was out of this world," Dr. Murdock told her.

"Well, my land o' livin!" Elizabeth murmured. "I'd never have thought that Gilbert woman could boil water without scorching it!"

Dr. Murdock laughed, and his arm drew Susan close.

"It was Susan who cooked dinner, Elizabeth!" he said. "And it was something to be proud of!"

Susan said laughingly, "Oh, Elizabeth had already thawed the steaks and marinated them. All I did was broil them and mix a salad."

"Well, of course I knew you could cook," Elizabeth said. "Glad you didn't all go hungry account of Sandy and me blowing our tops like we did."

She hesitated a moment and then

looked anxiously from Susan to Dr. Murdock.

"That's on the level, Doc, about the Cedars being turned into a hospital?" she asked.

"Don't you approve, Elizabeth?" He was obviously somewhat surprised.

"Oh, my land o' livin', yes! Not that it's any of my business, Doc, seeing the chief left you the place to do anything you wanted with," she answered. "It's just that I was wondering: will there be a place for Stepp here? We kinda promised him when we found him at the garage, if he'd come back he could stay. I know we didn't have no right to make him any such promise—"

"Don't be absurd, Elizabeth!" Susan cried, and Dr. Murdock echoed her.

"There'll always be a place at the Cedars for people who loved and served the chief as selflessly and as devotedly as you did, all of you, and you had a perfect right to promise him that he could stay," Dr. Murdock answered. "Why, with his experience taking care of the chief, Stepp will be invaluable in such a place."

"Well, now, I'm real glad to hear that," said Elizabeth. "We found him at the garage, and he was standing there and giving them a rough time, account of he had his own ideas about what they should be doing to the chief's car. He said he had the great-granddaddy of all hangovers and it sure had taught him a lesson. He wasn't ever going to take another drink as long as he lived. And d'you know something? I believe he really meant it! And wouldn't that be something?"

"I'm sure he meant it, Elizabeth, and we must all help him by believing in him and helping him," said Dr. Murdock quietly, "as the chief did, remember?"

"Sure," said Elizabeth, and heaved a deep sigh. "The chief sure worked hard to get Stepp straightened out. Reckon maybe he'd want us to keep that up, don't you?"

"Of course he would!" Dr. Murdock answered.

As though resenting the fact that he

had been kept out of the conversation for so long, Sandy asked grumpily, "Well, are you planning to sit here all night keeping Doc and Miss Susan up? Reckon maybe they're kinda tired don't you?"

Elizabeth glared at him as she sat back. "Well, go on; let's get home, then. See you in the morning, Miss Susan. And there'll be waffles for breakfast!" she announced and added, as the station wagon started, "Why don't you come up to breakfast, Doc? I'll have plenty of waffles for everybody."

"I'll take you up on that, Elizabeth," Dr. Murdock called as the station wagon went on its way.

"Oh, I'm so glad they came back," said Susan happily. "This has been their home for so long they'd be miserable anywhere else."

"Of course they would" Dr. Murdock answered. He drew her close and looked out over the sweep of lawn to the sea beyond; looked at the dark shadows of the cedars making ink blotches on the lawn in the star-shine. There was no moon, but the sky was so thickly sprinkled with stars that the air seemed luminous with their shimmering. "Nobody who had ever lived here could be happy anywhere else."

"I don't think so either," she assured him.

He looked down at her face, dimly illuminated by the light from the instrument panel of his car.

"Look, honey, you don't think maybe it will be too quiet here for you? I mean you won't miss living in a big city, with all the entertainment and amusements that are available there?" he asked.

Susan laughed that to scorn.

"Now just how much entertainment and amusement could a busy nurse find even in a big city?" she mocked him. "She has a day off every now and then, of course; but it has to go for shopping, for shampoos, for a million things that are by no means entertaining."

She cocked her head and looked up at him, and though he could not see her expression, there was a hint of laughter in her teasing voice.

"Dr. Murdock," she demanded, "are you by any chance trying to wiggle out of marrying me and bringing me to the Cedars to live?"

He laughed at the absurdity of that. Before he could answer, she went on firmly, "Because if you are, it will get you nowhere at all! I'm not the type to take kindly to being jilted, so don't try it!"

"Threatening me, are you?" His tone matched hers in its teasing quality.

"You're darned right I am! You just try to jilt me, mister, and the threats the Barfords made will sound like an invitation to a Sunday School picnic," she warned him.

"My, my, what a belligerent female!" he mocked her.

"Don't push me too far or you may find out how dangerous I am!"

She dissolved into unsteady laughter as he drew her close and hard against him and held her, his cheek against hers.

"It's going to be wonderful, isn't it, honey?" he asked after a long, lovely moment.

"Oh, so very wonderful! Bless Mr. Cantrell for bringing me here where I could meet you! Just think, if he hadn't I might never have known you!" She was appalled at the thought.

"Oh, I'd have found you, honey! You were set aside for me by some lovely miracle. I had to find you! But Mr. Cantrell made it easier." He drew a deep breath. "And some day soon, darling, *very* soon—"

"How about Sunday?" she suggested happily. "That's four days off! We can get our license by then, can't we?"

"Of course. We can do it here on the terrace, maybe, or would you rather we were married in church?"

"I think I'd rather be married here at the Cedars, with Elizabeth and Stepp and Sandy as our guests. Or would that be too small a wedding?" she asked.

"I've always understood that three people were all that were really essential for a wedding—him, her and the preacher-man!" Dr. Murdock teased her.

"Well, I just thought that, what with

your being such a popular man in the village—I saw today, remember?—they might all want to attend anything as important as your wedding," she pointed out.

"I'm afraid you're exaggerating my importance, sweetheart! And if there is anything in the world that two people alone have the right to arrange, it's their wedding, don't you think?" he suggested.

She drew a deep sigh and smiled in the dim light.

"I think that it's high time you and I said good night and you went home and got some sleep. And I'll do the same," she told him firmly.

He nodded as he cupped her chin in his palm and tilted her face upward for his kiss.

"Tomorrow is another day," he agreed.

"Tomorrow and tomorrow and tomorrow!" she echoed, her face radiant with the joy of the thought. "Oh, darling, think of all the lovely tomorrows that are ahead!"

"I'm thinking of them," said Dr.

Murdock huskily. "Three hundred and sixty-five of them every year for at least fifty years."

Susan laughed shakily. "Oh, at least fifty!"

It was a prospect so glorious that the very thought of it held them in silent rapture.

THE END

DOCTOR NAPIER'S NURSE
by Pauline Ash
When cousins Midge and Derry are entered as probationer nurses on the same day but at different hospitals they agree to exchange identities.

A GIRL LIKE JULIE
by Louise Ellis
Caroline absolutely adored Hugh Barrington, but then Julie Crane came into their lives. Julie was the kind of girl who attracts men without even trying.

COUNTRY DOCTOR
by Paula Lindsay
When Evan Richmond bought a practice in a remote country village he did not realise that a casual encounter would lead to the loss of his heart.

ENCORE
by Helga Moray
Craig and Janet realise that their true happiness lies with each other, but it is only under traumatic circumstances that they can be reunited.

NICOLETTE
by Ivy Preston
When Grant Alston came back into her life, Nicolette was faced with a dilemma. Should she follow the path of duty or the path of love?

THE GOLDEN PUMA
by Margaret Way
Catherine's time was spent looking after her father's Queensland farm. But what life was there without David, who wasn't interested in her?

HOSPITAL BY THE LAKE
by Anne Durham
Nurse Marguerite Ingleby was always ready to become personally involved with her patients, to the despair of Brian Field, the Senior Surgical Registrar, who loved her.

VALLEY OF CONFLICT
by David Farrell
Isolated in a hostel in the French Alps, Ann Russell sees her fiancé being seduced by a young girl. Then comes the avalanche that imperils their lives.

NURSE'S CHOICE
by Peggy Gaddis
A proposal of marriage from the incredibly handsome and wealthy Reagan was enough to upset any girl—and Brooke Martin was no exception.

A DANGEROUS MAN
by Anne Goring
Photographer Polly Burton was on safari in Monbasa when she met enigmatic Leon Hammond. But unpredictability was the name of the game where Leon was concerned.

PRECIOUS INHERITANCE
by Joan Moules
Karen's new life working for an authoress took her from Sussex to a foreign airstrip and a kidnapping; to a real life adventure as gripping as any in the books she typed.

VISION OF LOVE
by Grace Richmond
When Kathy takes over the run-down country kennels she finds Alec Stinton, a local vet, very helpful. But their friendship arouses bitter jealousy and a tragedy seems inevitable.

CRUSADING NURSE
by Jane Converse
It was handsome Dr. Corbett who opened Nurse Susan Leighton's eyes and who set her off on a lonely crusade against some powerful enemies and a shattering struggle against the man she loved.

WILD ENCHANTMENT
by Christina Green
Rowan's agreeable new boss had a dream of creating a famous perfume using her precious Silverstar, but Rowan's plans were very different.

DESERT ROMANCE
by Irene Ord
Sally agrees to take her sister Pam's place as La Chartreuse the dancer, but she finds out there is more to it than dyeing her hair red and looking like her sister.

HEART OF ICE
by Marie Sidney

How was January to know that not only would the warmth of the Swiss people thaw out her frozen heart, but that she too would play her part in helping someone to live again?

LUCKY IN LOVE
by Margaret Wood

Melanie, companion-secretary to the wealthy Laura Duxford, had lost her heart to Laura's son, Julian. Someone was trying to get Laura—a compulsive gambler—thrown out of the Casino, someone who would even resort to murder.

NURSE TO PRINCESS JASMINE
by Lilian Woodward

Nick's surgeon brother, Tom, performs an operation on an Arabian princess, and she invites Tom, Nick and his fiancé to Omander, where a web of deceit and intrigue closes about the three young people.

THE WAYWARD HEART
by Eileen Barry

Disaster-prone Katherine's nickname was "Kate Calamity". She was a good natured girl, but her boss went too far with an outrageous proposal, because of her latest disaster, she could not refuse.

FOUR WEEKS IN WINTER
by Jane Donnelly

Tessa wasn't looking forward to going back to her old home town and meeting Paul Mellor again—she had made a fool of herself over him once before. But was Orme Jared's solution to her problem likely to be the right one?

SURGERY BY THE SEA
by Sheila Douglas

Medical student Meg hadn't really wanted to leave London and her boyfriend to go and work with a G.P. on the Welsh coast for the summer, although the job had its compensations. But Owen Roberts was certainly not one of them!